# Blood On The Range

## by
## Christopher Reynolds

Publisher's Note:

This is a work of fiction. All names, characters, places, and
events are the work of the author's imagination.

Any resemblance to real persons, places, or events is
coincidental.

Solstice Publishing - http://www.solsticeempire.com/

# Chapter One

The town of Langston sat between the Tongue and Powder Rivers in present-day southeastern Montana just a dozen or so miles north of the now Wyoming border. It would come as a surprise to those who lived nearby in the latter part of the 19th Century if it were still standing today. The spring of 1881 saw the beginning of a war among cattle ranchers that would cost many lives, both livestock and people.

T.L. Langston had come to the Montana territory in late '60 for a fresh start in wide open country. A Mississippi cotton plantation owner, Langston saw the writing on the wall concerning the coming war and sold out his entire operation. With his pockets full of money, freedom on his mind, and the urge for something new to call his own, he claimed land in the territory that would become the town that carried his name.

Building a town is no easy feat, but Langston's desire to be the boss again far outweighed the challenges ahead of him. With many recruitment trips down toward Mexico and around the western territories he was able to attract plenty of cattlemen willing to brave the elements and other typical perils that were ever-present on the drive, including raids from Indians. Through their perseverance they rode on and managed to settle Langston and its surrounding land.

It doesn't take much talk of free land with plenty of grass and opportunity to attract cattlemen. And where the cattle go, so does the money. People have to eat and beef is good. But cowpunchers don't want to spend all their time around cattle. That's where the entertainment needed to fill their free time they had come in.

Within a matter of a year and a half, Langston was booming considering its northern proximity to other previous settlements. Its layout was simple, with just two streets crossing each other and dividing the town into four separate quadrants. The edge of town lay just off where the railroad tracks were to come, in Mr. Langston's plans. The town's popularity grew to the point that the railroad to Butte officially added a depot to accommodate the town.

The town's arrangement of only two streets was not by chance, but by grand design. It was laid out in the shape of a cross as Mr. Langston was quite a religious fellow. Despite his convictions, he understood that the night life would be a significant aspect of the cowboys' lives so his town must have these elements. Therefore, such establishments as would offer these types of accommodations were allowed, but at the far end of town, a rule that would change in later days.

In fact, closest to the tracks and station was Langston's oldest building, the church. Its first pastor, Will Tucker, took the position in 1861 and held it for six and a half years until he died in the pulpit from a heart attack in the midst of a fiery sermon. Mr. Langston himself had to be eulogized by townsfolk as a bout of pneumonia took his life just weeks after the preacher's death.

The passing of these two men sent the town into a downward spiral for the better part of a year. With its moral center dead and gone, wickedness began to overtake the town's goodness. In eight months' time, there had been seven murders within town limits, five more than had been committed in the town's entire previous history. One of these murders had actually been the sheriff at the hands of his own deputy, who then became sheriff himself.

Langston's future looked bleak; acts of violence became the new norm. Coupled with the sheriff having achieved the position by ill-gotten means and running roughshod, his lack of control over the town's lawlessness was causing Langston's once sterling reputation to lose its luster.

However, the light at the end of the tunnel began to come into view upon the arrival of a new preacher, Montgomery Cole, a friend of the late preacher of Langston. The religious folk of the town were more than eager to welcome Cole after hearing of his correspondence and great friendship with their beloved former pastor. Cole had traveled with Tucker evangelizing across much of the south for a few years. Upon receiving news of his brother in ministry's death, Cole felt that the Lord had called him to minister to Tucker's former parishioners. By February of 1869, Cole had been fully installed as the minister of the Church of Langston.

With a new preacher in town, some of the men of the town began to turn away from its carnal offerings and back into the waiting arms of the church. The reintroduction of church services was enough to begin to sway the balance in the way of good in the great battle against evil. Apparently, being held accountable for one's sins is enough to make many men shy away from that frowned upon way of living. In fact, the sheriff himself even repented and was voted upon almost unanimously to continue his duties in a town meeting, a position he held for another three years.

Two more arrivals that strengthened the backbone of Langston were that of cattle ranching families, the Barkhouses and Kaysers, led by their respective patriarchs, Talmadge and Giles. The two men had served together in the War Between the States where they had formed a strong bond, and even though they had never gone in as partners, both men felt a strong allegiance to one another. They'd started their individual ranching operations and their families remained close, with Talmadge's only daughter, Claire, even marrying one of Giles' sons, Luke.

Both men and their families held steadfast religious beliefs and were quickly welcomed by Pastor Cole and his congregation. They were viewed as beacons of the town and its surrounding area, always standing up for what they believed. Each Sunday morning saw them loading up their wagons and making the trek from their nearby homesteads into town for the church services.

For nearly 10 years, Langston continued to thrive without any hint of dissent. Not unlike any other town in the latter 19th century, Langston had its share of issues from time to time, but for the most part it was about as peaceful as a town could be under the circumstances. A decade of peace and prosperity would begin to unravel in the spring of '78 when a new cattle rancher made his way to Langston. This first sign of possible trouble came about with the arrival of Pastor Montgomery Cole's brother, Murphy.

The preacher's other brothers Milo, Marvin, and Melvin were soon to follow Murphy.

Despite some setbacks several years before his arrival in Langston, Murphy had managed to reestablish his cattle operation to its former strength, and even become stronger. In the approximately three years that he'd been in Langston, Murphy Cole had gained few friends but much wealth.

Backed by the funds of their brother Murphy, and the power that money brought, all three brothers had gained prominent positions in town. In their short time there in Langston, Milo had taken over as sheriff, Marvin had opened a new mercantile store, and Melvin had bought the town's saloon.

# Chapter Two

"Brothers and sisters," Pastor Montgomery Cole began. "In the eleventh chapter of the book of Isaiah, the Good Book tells us 'the wolf also shall dwell with the lamb, and the leopard shall lie down with the kid; and the calf and the young lion and the fatling together; and a little child shall lead them.' This is in the sixth verse."

He stepped out from behind the pulpit and looked into the eyes of several members of the congregation, which nearly filled the two sections of seven handmade pews. Among the faithful, packed into their ordinary spot in the second pew to Cole's right, sat Talmadge Barkhouse and his family: his wife Belle and his sons Lake, Asa, Augustus, Avery, Chauncey, and the youngest, Orel.

Directly across from them sat Giles and Judith Kayser, along with their own children, Daniel, Simon, Mary and Martha. The married couple of Luke and Claire Kayser, formerly Barkhouse, joined his family.

"Yes, there is coming a day," the preacher continued. "When these things will be."

His passion is met with a chorus of "amens".

"But for now, we must be wary of these wolves. They are instruments of the Devil used to devour us."

One such wolf was sitting on the center aisle end of the back right pew. It was none other than the pastor's brother, Murphy. Murphy was a big man, several inches over six feet and broad across the shoulders. Age had added a few pounds to his middle, but he was still an imposing figure nonetheless. While others around him praised God, Murphy Cole sat stock still as if the appearance of Jesus himself wouldn't excite him in the least.

With the sermon finished, most of the crowd stood about the front steps of the church fellowshipping. For some of them, this was their only day in town for the week that wasn't spent tending to business. To one side stood the respective owners of the three largest nearby cattle ranches, Murphy Cole, Talmadge Barkhouse, and Giles Kayser. Talmadge's height matched that of Cole, but he had a wiry frame that seemed to hold nothing but muscle. While not a small man in his own right, Giles seemed rather diminutive standing with these two.

"That brother of yours sure can preach, eh Murphy?" Giles asked.

"Sure," Murphy replied dryly.

"Say, where's Preston this morning?" Talmadge added.

Preston was Murphy's only son, the heir to the empire so to speak.

"He's a little under the weather this morning."

"Hope it's nothing serious," Talmadge remarked.

"Oh I'm sure it's nothing. Probably just didn't want to get out of bed to be honest."

As he said this, Montgomery Cole stepped over and joined the conversation.

"Wonderful sermon pastor," Giles said as he grabbed the preacher's hand and shook it heartily.

"Yes sir. Another fine one." Talmadge interjected, shaking his hand as well.

"Well thank you Giles, Talmadge. I owe it all to the Lord."

Montgomery looked to his brother, perhaps for more adulation. Murphy met his gaze but said nothing. Instead, he turned his attention elsewhere.

"Excuse me gentlemen. I have some business to attend to." Murphy stated without even a slight tip of his hat as he headed off down the street into town.

As the three men watched him walk away, Talmadge piped up.

"Hard to figure that brother of yours."

"Murphy?" Montgomery asked. "He's ain't hard to figure at all. He just don't like anybody."

The trio laughed at this.

"True enough I guess."

"Say Rev," Giles said. "How come your other brothers never come to services?"

"They're too busy."

"They couldn't take a little time off on the Lord's day?"

"That's the thing. Ain't the Lord says they're too busy for church. It's Murphy."

"He really runs the family, huh?" Talmadge asked.

"My brothers, yes. I'm the oldest but he's pretty much always been the leader. I never was a fan of his leadership so I followed my calling and left."

"And he followed you," Talmadge added.

The pastor looked at both of his friends and congregation members and laughed a little.

"Yep, pretty much. He followed me and they followed him."

\*\*\*

At the Barkhouse home that afternoon, the men of the family gathered around the dining table to dig in on a feast of shoulder roast from a freshly slaughtered cow and crispy fried chicken from off the yard along with vegetables that had been stored from the previous year's harvest. This meal had been prepared with a great deal of effort and love by the family matriarch, Belle. On days like today, the simple ranching family felt as if they were kings and a queen dining at the royal table.

"Won't you say grace, Tal?" Belle asked her husband as she finally took her seat at the opposite end of the table from him.

"Of course," he replied, smiling as he looked into the soft brown eyes of the woman he loved, the woman who had given him six strong sons and a beautiful daughter who was currently having Sunday dinner with her in-laws.

"Let's bow our heads."

They grabbed each other's hands in solidarity and bowed their heads as Talmadge prayed.

"Dear Heavenly father," he began. "We thank you for this wonderful meal that we are about to enjoy. Thank you for the hands that prepared it and the ability to grow the necessary harvests to have it. Your grace and mercy have not gone unnoticed. Amen."

"Amen," everyone else added.

As they happily passed around dishes and filled their plates with hard-earned food, the Barkhouses had no idea of the wheels that had been put into motion that would change their lives forever. All while they attended church with the man who had ordered the plans just hours earlier.

# Chapter Three

"Is it done?" Murphy Cole asked his right hand man Gene Cook as he entered the ranch house.

A simple nod told Cole that it was. The "it" being the theft of some Barkhouse cattle.

"We cut out probably 75 head, maybe 100," Preston Cole, Murphy's only son added as he followed Cook in. His mother had died in childbirth so he had a unique relationship with his father. Murphy wasn't very tough on Preston, but he didn't have to be. In Preston's eyes, Murphy could do no wrong so he was more than happy to oblige any orders his father made.

"You start on the eastern side to take away any thoughts of it being us that done it?" Murphy asked from his big easy chair, a smoldering cigar nestled under his big mustache and a glass of whiskey in his hand.

"Yes sir, just like you said."

"Good. Curtis cooked up some grub when you boys are cleaned up and ready to eat."

Curtis, or Black Curtis as most called him, was the lone black man in the Cole outfit. He did a little bit of anything that needed to be done around the ranch whether it be actual ranching, or cooking and cleaning. If it needed doing, Black Curtis could and would do it.

\*\*\*

The next morning found the Barkhouse men conducting their normal beginning of the week head count on cattle: Lake and Orel east toward the Powder, Asa and Chauncey west to the Tongue, and Avery and Augustus taking the middle ground. Upon his arrival at their meeting point,

Talmadge immediately noticed the absence of his oldest and youngest sons.

"Where's Lake and Orel?" he asked no one in particular as he rode up on his gray stud.

"Haven't seen or heard anything," Asa offered.

"Hmm," Talmadge pondered, rubbing his stubbly chin.

"Reckon we need to ride that way, Pa?" Augustus asked.

"No need," Asa chimed back in. "Here they come."

Over a nearby ridge came the boys at a hurried pace. Even at better than a hundred yards away, Talmadge could see a look of concern on Lake's face. He spurred his horse on towards his sons.

"What's the matter, son?" Talmadge asked his oldest.

"We got cattle missing, at least 80 head."

"Could you tell where they headed?"

"We tracked them a ways toward the river but we lost the trail just shy of the first creek and couldn't pick it back up."

"Any horse tracks?"

"Some, but they're all muddled up," Lake nodded.

Talmadge sat back in his saddle, thinking for a moment. He looked at the terrain about him as if it may hold the answers he sought.

"Tell you what," he began. "Lake, you and Orel ride out to the Kaysers'. See if Giles has seen anything of our cattle and we'll put fresh eyes on these tracks."

"Sure thing Pa," Lake replied.

He and Orel set out for the Kayser ranch as Talmadge and his other sons headed east toward where the last sign of the cattle had been seen.

\*\*\*

Giles Kayser had a dozen or so calves corralled up behind the house for branding when he saw the Barkhouse brothers approaching. A calf bellowed as steam from his fresh brand rose in the air.

"Alright, let him up," he told Daniel, pleased with the clarity of the Circle K on the calf's rump.

Daniel took his weight off the calf and he came up in a hurry, nearly running into the fire for the iron. A swift kick to the rear end set him right and he joined his other freshly marked comrades.

"That's half. We'll take a break and see what these boys want," Giles said as he wiped the sweat from his brow. It was an uncharacteristically warm day for early spring in Montana.

"Howdy, boys."

Lake tipped his hat as he and his brother rode up to the fence and dismounted.

"Morning, Mr. Kayser," Lake responded as he extended his hand. "Warm, ain't it?"

Lake himself was shiny with sweat from the morning's work and ride over.

"Sure is," Giles said. "What brings you boys this way?"

"Well we got some cattle missing, probably 80 or 100 head. Was wondering if you'd seen 'em by chance."

"Simon and Luke went out on a head count this morning. I'll check with them."

"Simon!" he yelled out toward the house. "Luke!"

In just a moment, Luke emerged from the horse barn with a pitchfork in hand.

"Yea, Pa?" he hollered back.

"Come here a minute."

Luke planted the pitchfork in the ground and headed over to the others at the corral. At the same time, Simon came from around the house and started over as well.

"What's going on Pa?" Luke asked.

"We got some cattle missing," Lake spoke up.

"You boys see any sign of them this morning while you were out with the herd?" Giles asked.

Both Kaysers shook their heads.

"Sure didn't."

Orel, who was only 13, stood by his horse. He was both the youngest and shyest of the Barkhouses. He'd rather blend into his surroundings than talk to anybody other than maybe Lake or his mother.

"Last sign we had of them was heading back this way but a little further north," Lake added.

"I didn't see any sign at all, Lake. Everything was on the up and up this way," Simon said.

"Well if y'all happen to see hide or hair of 'em, give us a shout. I'm hoping they got separated and wandered off. Pa's out there tracking now."

"If anybody took them cattle, your Pa will figure it out. He's the nearest thing to an Indian I've ever seen on a track," Giles noted.

"We'll get out of your hair. No use in your fire dying on account of idle talk," Lake said, noticing the fading heat of the branding iron fire.

Giles smiled and looked back at the fire for himself.

"She is getting pretty weak. We'll have our eyes peeled boys. Y'all have a good one."

"Much appreciated," Lake replied as he swung up into his saddle.

Orel followed suit and with a tip of their hats, the eldest and youngest Barkhouses set out for home and the Kaysers got back to work.

By the creek edge where Lake and Orel had lost the trail of the missing cattle, Talmadge led his horse slowly by the reins as he stooped over the tracks. In a soft sandy spot, he took notice of some double-trod horse tracks. His knowledge of tracking told him that it'd been done intentionally, no doubt about it.

"You reckon somebody stole them cattle, Pa?" Augustus asked as he approached his father.

"It's sure starting to look that way," he answered.

"Crow maybe?"

"No, I don't believe so. These horses was shoed."

Talmadge stood to his feet and faced his four sons that were with him. Having joined Augustus, the other brothers studied their father's face. It was like looking at an older version of themselves as they all looked like Talmadge. They all had the same facial features and tall, slender build. Lake did too for that matter.

Orel was the only exception. He favored Talmadge quite a bit facially, but his build was completely different. He was several inches shorter than any of his brothers had been at his age with broad, powerful shoulders like Belle's father. And even though he was six years or so younger than his youngest brother Chauncey, he was already just as strong as any of them.

"What you thinking, Pa?" Avery asked.

"That whoever done this was mighty careful about not leaving any legible sign. Something don't add up."

"So you don't think it was rustlers either?" Asa added.

"Not the typical kind anyhow."

Talmadge's gut told him that there was some sort of message hidden in these tracks, or lack thereof. Somebody had been careful, too careful for his liking. Yes, it was a message alright. But what was the message and who sent it?

# Chapter Four

When nearly a week had gone by without any hint of where his cattle had wandered off to, Talmadge Barkhouse set out one morning for the ranch of Murphy Cole. He had no idea that a message had been sent through the disappearance of his cattle or that this message had been sent by the man whose home he was bound for.

At the large house of the sprawling Cole ranch, Murphy was more than welcoming to his visitor. Probably too welcoming if Talmadge had thought about it, but Murphy was always friendlier in his own domain where he felt more comfortable and in charge.

The Cole house was a large log structure with two floors and double-thick walls. It had a large den with a fireplace and handsome furnishings that welcomed you in as you entered the front door. Each of Murphy's seven head of men had a bedroom of their own, as well as his son Preston. Three or four acres of land were fenced in as a yard around the home.

Murphy Cole stood leaned up on his fence beside the gate, puffing on one of his favorite cigars as Talmadge approached on horseback.

"Good morning," Murphy said enthusiastically.

Talmadge looked less than excited to see the happier than usual Cole.

"Morning," Talmadge replied dryly, dismounting his horse and tying him to the fence.

He stepped over to where Murphy stood with his hand extended to shake. Talmadge examined it momentarily as if it might be some sort of trap awaiting him before accepting it.

"You seem mighty chipper this morning," he remarked.

"Too fine of a morning to be so sour," Murphy replied as he blew a big puff of smoke.

Talmadge looked into Murphy's eyes and he just stared right back. His dark brown eyes lacked any kind of sparkle. Even when he was happy or amused, you could never tell it in his eyes. They appeared to just be dead pools of nothing.

As they broke their stare, Black Curtis stepped out of the front door.

"Murphy. Talmadge. Can I get you fellas anything? Coffee?"

Murphy looked at his guest, but he only shook his head.

"No thank you, Curt. We're alright," Murphy responded without ever looking in his direction.

Curtis spun right around on his heels and disappeared back where he came from as Murphy set his mind back on his previous conversation.

"So what brings you here Talmadge? I'm assuming by your demeanor this wasn't a pleasurable trip."

"No, you're right. It's not."

"So what is it?" Murphy prodded.

"We had some cattle get gone."

"They just wandered off?"

"Appears not. I found horse tracks, but not enough to make any sense of."

"No?" Murphy asked, sounding surprised. "Thought you could track most anything."

This condescending remark wasn't met well by Talmadge.

"I reckon not," he replied. "I was just wondering if you'd seen anything of them or maybe they'd got mixed in with some of yours."

"No, everything over here is Cole stock," he lied.

Talmadge studied his fellow rancher, trying to read him. It was to no avail as Murphy Cole had the damnedest poker face he'd ever seen on a man. He'd have better luck getting a straight answer from his cattle. But then again, maybe it was a straight answer. Who was to know?

"Well," Talmadge began. "I won't take up any more of your time. I've got work to do anyway."

With this said, Talmadge begrudgingly shook Murphy's hand again and mounted his horse. With a tip of his hat, he headed for home.

"I'll let you know if I see anything of your cattle," Murphy called out to him as he rode away.

Talmadge only threw up his hand in parting. He furrowed his brow in annoyance with this man he'd never much cared for. Whether he'd been telling the truth or not, Talmadge told himself that nothing said he had to like him.

\*\*\*

Less than a mile out from the Cole ranch, Talmadge began to feel as if he was being followed. As he came upon a rise, a quick look back over his shoulder told him he was right. At that distance, he couldn't tell who it was so he tucked himself away in some scrub brush just as he came down the other side of the hill.

It didn't take long to find out who'd been pursuing him. It was Black Curtis. Talmadge could tell Curtis was trying to discern where he'd gone. When he had him at about 50 yards, Talmadge started his horse out into the open, his hand on his revolver that lay cocked in his lap.

"Curt," he said sharply.

Curtis nearly jumped out of his skin, startled by Talmadge's voice.

"Talmadge," he responded shakily. "You nearly scared me to death."

"How come you following me? Murphy send you to look after me?"

By now, Talmadge had ridden up beside Curtis. He didn't expect any trouble, but if it were to arise, he'd rather it happen in close quarters.

"No. I come to tell you something," he said, his voice a little calmer.

"Yea?"

"It was Murphy got your cattle."

Talmadge was surprised even though he knew he shouldn't be.

"You sure?"

"Positive," Curtis said. "Heard 'em talking 'bout it from the kitchen the other night."

"And how come you telling me?" Talmadge asked, his eyes wide.

"Ain't right a man stealing what belongs to another man. I got to go though. Don't want Murphy suspecting nothing."

No sooner had the words left his mouth, Black Curtis clicked his tongue, heading his horse back in the direction he'd come from.

Talmadge watched him briefly, trying to digest this new information. Was this all a smokescreen? Had Murphy sent him to say that for some odd reason? Surely not. Curtis was a good man as far as he knew. Which then again, so was Murphy Cole. He had no reason to suspect him of rustling other than the fact that he didn't like him. He had seemed awful happy to see him though, hadn't he?

As he rode home, Talmadge didn't know anything for sure. All he knew was that he didn't like the way this whole situation made him feel.

# Chapter Five

That night, Talmadge laid in bed beside his wife unable to sleep. He pondered everything that had happened in the last week and wondered just how it had come to this. His Colt in the gun belt hung beside his bed, a place it hadn't been since tensions were high with nearby Crow Indians. This bothered Belle, who also was also awake, unbeknownst to her husband.

Talmadge wondered why Murphy had waited so long to make his move, if it was him that had stolen those cattle. He had no reason to doubt what Black Curtis had told him, but he didn't want to believe it. He just wanted to be at peace. There'd been enough fighting in his life.

"Tal," Belle whispered softly. "What's bothering you?"

His heart skipped a beat as her voice broke the silence. He turned his head slightly to take a look at his wife in the light from the window without making eye contact.

"Nothing," he lied.

Belle didn't appreciate his dishonesty in the least. She sat up in the bed and stared at him but he wouldn't meet her gaze.

"Look at me, Talmadge," she commanded.

She rarely used his whole name, but when she did he knew she meant business. He sat up in bed beside her and looked her in the eyes. He could tell she was deeply concerned. There was no hiding it. He probably told her more than most men would tell their wives, but he knew she could handle it. She'd raised six children on her own while he'd been at war and she'd been with him every step of the way from Kentucky, to Arkansas, then way up here without complaint. There was no doubt that Belle Foster Barkhouse was a strong woman.

"I rode over to Murphy Cole's today, told him about the cattle," he said.

"Did he say something to upset you?" she asked.

"No. He didn't say much of anything really."

This answer both surprised and confused her.

"Well what's bothering you then?"

Talmadge sighed as he forced himself to tell his wife the truth of what was weighing on his mind.

"On the way home, Black Curtis caught up with me," he told her before stopping.

"And?" she urged.

"He claims Cole's responsible for them cattle getting gone. Said he overheard him talking about it with his men."

Belle's eyes opened wide and Talmadge tried to discern her reaction. She tried to play it cool, but he could hear the tension in her voice when she responded.

"You don't believe him?"

"I do. That's the problem."

Both of them sat in silence attempting to make sense of the situation they found themselves in.

"Curtis seems to be an honest man as far as I know," she said.

"That's what worries me. I've got no reason to not believe him, but I wish I did."

"Just doesn't make sense."

"Nope," he said. "The timing don't add up at all. He's been here, what, nigh on three years? Why start trouble now?"

Belle didn't have the answers to the questions her husband was asking and he didn't expect her to. He just needed her to listen, so listen she did.

Neither one of them knew what to say so they just sat together quietly until Belle struck a match and lit the lamp beside their bed. In the dim light of their room, she began to flip through her Bible. When she came to Isaiah 11:6 she stopped and read to herself.

"What ya reading?" Talmadge asked, glancing over at the pages.

"Isaiah 11:6," she said.

"Oh yeah?"

"Yea. Monty preached on it Sunday."

"Yeah he did," Talmadge added.

"You know Preston wasn't with Murphy."

The wheels began to turn in Talmadge's mind as the picture came into focus.

"Murphy seemed to be in even more of a hurry than normal. Said he had business to attend to."

Belle and Talmadge looked at each other realizing, rather unfortunately, that the information they had been given was most likely true. Talmadge just shook his head.

"I just don't understand."

"Me either," Belle added.

"It's not like he needs to put me out of business. There's more than enough room for three ranches here."

"And with the railroad coming through and having a weekly train back and forth to Butte," Belle chimed in.

"He's already got the biggest ranch by far. We're just trying to make a living here."

"It's the devil, Tal. Nothing but pure meanness."

By this point, both Barkhouses were steaming, but Belle more so than her husband. They'd worked hard to get to this point. She hadn't dragged her children across the country to have everything they'd worked for snatched from them when it was really paying off.

"What are we going to do?" she asked.

"I reckon I've got to go to the sheriff about it," he answered.

Belle wanted this to be handled by the book, but she didn't know whether or not that was possible when the sheriff was brother to the man who stole their cattle.

"You think that's a good idea? With Milo being a Cole, I mean," she noted

"I don't know. But I can't let this go unanswered."

"And I wouldn't expect you to."

"I guess I'll go see him tomorrow."

"On Sunday?" Belle asked incredulously.

"After church," he replied quickly. "Look, I hate to handle business on Sunday as bad as you do, but it'll save me a trip into town. And with Murphy rustling cattle, we've got to be with the herd as much as possible. I can't take any chances."

She only nodded. She didn't like the idea of tending to business on the Lord's Day. That was just the type of thing Murphy Cole would do. Talmadge was right though. It had to be done.

"Tomorrow it is then," she said before kissing Talmadge and blowing out the light from the lamp.

They both laid their heads back down and tried to get some-much needed sleep, but it didn't find them.

\*\*\*

As soon as church was dismissed the next day, Talmadge went to see Milo Cole, the sheriff.

"I'll be back soon," he called to his family as he strode down the street.

Murphy Cole stood out front of the church with his hands in his pockets watching Talmadge walk away. He wondered what was so important that Talmadge Barkhouse of all people would be conducting business on a Sunday. Regardless, he'd know by tonight what it was one way or another. Not much happened in or around Langston that he didn't know about, whether it was any of his business or not.

Upon his arrival at the jail, Talmadge was greeted by Milo and his three deputies, all of whom were in various states of relaxation. Chief Deputy Warren Clement was stretched out on one of the bunks in the cell that sat to the left of the door, Roger Nelson's chin was nearly resting on his chest, and Jasper Maxwell had his feet propped up on the desk along with his boss.

"Howdy, Talmadge," Milo said with a bit of enthusiasm.

Milo looked a good deal like Murphy, but acted completely opposite. He was a jovial man who loved conversation. More of his time was spent talking to townspeople rather than on being an actual lawman. Everyone knew he was a bought and paid-for sheriff with hand-picked deputies other than Clement who was an aging holdover from the last regime.

"It's good to see our money is going to pay such a hard-working group of lawmen," Talmadge remarked sarcastically.

"We've got a lot on our hands, Mr. Barkhouse," Milo replied as he dropped his feet to the floor and sat up straight. "Just four men policing a town and enough surrounding area to hold three cattle ranches stretches us pretty thin."

"I can tell. I've had trouble with my cattle going missing and haven't heard from any of you."

Talmadge took a seat in the only empty chair across from Milo. For the first time since he'd arrived, the three deputies began paying attention to Talmadge.

Milo's friendly demeanor turned sour hurriedly as his brow furrowed.

"Well if we're not made aware of a problem, we can't rightly help you," he barked.

"Not everyone has time to come into town and find you or one of your deputies when they should be out patrolling. Some of us have work to do," Talmadge snapped right back.

He didn't know what had come over him. He'd come down here with every intention of simply making Milo aware of the issue as politely as possible. That's just who he was. But now, sitting here look at Milo, he knew that he knew the truth of the situation. His ability to blatantly feign ignorance infuriated Talmadge.

"What are you trying to say?" Milo asked less confidently.

Clement's face held a scowl that didn't go unnoticed by Talmadge. Milo's other deputies seemed none too pleased with what was being insinuated as well.

"What I'm saying is we've got cattle thieves out here taking our livelihood, and the men who are paid to handle such issues don't have time to make it out of town to do any real law work," Talmadge said, growing more and more agitated.

"I don't think I like your tone," Milo replied.

"And I don't like losing money."

Milo glared at Talmadge, but couldn't hold his stare when the angry rancher refused to be intimidated. The sheriff glanced around at his deputies for help.

"How 'bout the other ranches? They lose any cattle too?" Maxwell piped up.

"No. Just us."

Milo's attitude turned to condescension.

"Well maybe you just misplaced them," he said with a grin.

This attempt at humor drew a chorus of laughter from the deputies, but Talmadge wasn't amused in the least. He stood quickly from his chair and pounded his fist on Milo's desk. His voice was fierce and guttural when it left his mouth.

"I don't find any of this funny. Just do your damn job!"

It was not like Talmadge to use such language, especially on a Sunday. He was just that mad.

Roger Nelson leapt to his feet, but Milo quickly positioned himself between the two men. He didn't like Talmadge's tone either, but Milo knew that they had Murphy on their side and that meant a lot with affairs such as this.

"We'll get right on that," Milo told Talmadge, smiling as he restrained Nelson.

Talmadge had had all he could stand of being in the presence of this group of good for nothing lawmen. He turned for the door and headed outside, hurling one final remark as he left.

"Maybe you should ask your brother."

With that, he was gone, slamming the jail door shut behind him.

"What was that supposed to mean?" Nelson asked Milo.

Milo only shrugged as he sat back in his chair. He now knew that Talmadge knew that his brother was behind those cattle going missing. Like him or not, Talmadge was not one to say things without meaning behind them.

# Chapter Six

"He knows," were the first words out of Milo's mouth when Murphy asked him how things were.

At least once a week, and always on Sunday nights, the Cole men gathered for supper at Murphy's house. Murphy, Milo, Marvin, and Melvin that is. Not that Montgomery didn't associate with his brothers and nephew, but he wasn't invited to these meetings and with good reason. This is where the discussions concerning Murphy's plans to take control of Langston and everything surrounding it took place.

"Who knows what?" Murphy asked while puffing on a cigar, his dessert of choice after enjoying a big meal as they just had.

"Talmadge knows about the cattle. That you're responsible for the cattle of his that's gone missing."

Murphy cocked his head to the side a bit and looked over at his brother. He removed his cigar and blew out a big puff of smoke. His attention turned to it as he watched it dissipate before turning once again to Milo.

"What makes you say that?"

"He came into the jail talking about it today."

"So that's where he was off to in such a hurry after church. He said I did it?"

"Well, no," Milo answered. "But he said I should ask you about it."

In the kitchen, Black Curtis' ears perked up. The Coles had no idea he was even anywhere around still. The last they'd seen of him after he cooked their supper was him heading out the back door, but he'd slipped back in. Nobody but a Cole was let in on these meetings, not even Gene.

"So how's he know?" Murphy asked Milo.

Milo shrugged.

"Y'all heard any talk about it?" he asked his other brothers and Preston.

"This is the first I've heard of it," Marvin said.

"Nothing at the saloon," Melvin chimed in.

"Nope," Preston added.

Black Curtis made a show of opening and closing the back door as if he was just reentering the house.

"Mr. Murphy," he called from the kitchen. "You want I should put on some coffee?"

As he poked his head around the corner into the room, he was not met by friendly faces.

"No, Curtis," Murphy growled. "You know better than to be in here during our family meeting."

"Yes sir. I apologize," Curtis said, all the while backpedaling through the kitchen and out the backdoor.

Back at the table, Murphy sat back in his seat, rolling that big cigar in his big, meaty hands. He was studying his ash when Marvin spoke up.

"It's just as well he finds out now. He was gonna find out eventually."

Murphy mulled it over and nodded.

"Yea," Preston said. "Long as he don't go running his mouth to everybody around."

"Once the chips start to fall, I don't give a damn who knows," Murphy said. "Fear's a useful weapon in itself. I just want to know where the leak is."

They sat in silence for a few moments until Preston coughed a little. His father looked at him to see what this was about. Preston raised his eyebrows and turned his eyes in the direction of the kitchen as he spoke.

"Maybe…"

Murphy raised his own eyebrows as he considered this idea.

"Curtis?" he asked.

"It's possible," Preston replied.

"He does spend a lot of time around here," Murphy said thoughtfully. "Maybe he overheard something."

"And he was in here when he knew he shouldn't be," Milo added.

Murphy just nodded his head in agreement before looking to Preston.

"I'm gonna send him out with y'all more for a while. You stick close to him, you and Gene. See if he gives up anything."

"Yes sir."

"Whether Curtis is the leak or not, we'll find it. And you know what you do to a leak when you find it?"

"Plug it," Marvin answered.

"That's right."

***

When a few weeks had gone by without incident, Talmadge began to grow hopeful that his issue with Murphy Cole was behind him. Maybe his outburst at the jail had caused Murphy to reconsider his plan of action. There was no doubt that Milo had told his brother exactly what had happened. Rustling was a hanging offense and Talmadge didn't like the fact that Cole and his men would get away with it, but he would just have to be if it helped avoid further conflict.

Talmadge had almost allowed himself to relax, but the findings of an afternoon out with the cattle squashed any hopes of that.

"Pa!" Asa called, waving Talmadge over. "You need to see this!"

Talmadge trotted over on his horse the 50 or so yards to the edge of the ravine where his son stood.

"Look," he said as he pointed down.

Having ridden over and gotten off of his horse, Talmadge looked down the 30 some feet to the bottom of the ravine. What he saw there put a knot in his stomach and a fiery hate in his heart.

Below them laid a dozen or more Barkhouse cows, dead. The dug up ground on the ledge they stood on told them these cattle had been driven off the side.

"We've got to get down there and check them out," Talmadge said.

As he and Asa mounted up, Lake and Orel rode up to them. Lake could see the troubled look on his father's face immediately.

"What's going on?" he asked.

"Look for yourself," Talmadge answered, pointing to the ledge.

Lake and Orel eased over and peeked down into the ravine.

"Christ!" Orel exclaimed.

"Orel!" his father scolded.

Orel dropped his head, ashamed.

"Let's go," Talmadge instructed, leading the way west to find a more favorable grade to ease down.

It took them nearly a quarter of a mile to find a suitable slope to ride into the ravine. As they worked toward where their dead cattle were, a multitude of horse tracks became evident in the sandier ground.

"They didn't even try to hide it this time," Lake remarked as they eased along, studying the tracks as they went.

The boys chattered a bit among themselves, but Talmadge rode silently ahead. It wasn't that there wasn't anything that he wanted to say, there was just too much too begin. He'd always been honest and he thought that most people around here were too. Even Murphy seemed honest. Unfriendly most of the time, sure, but honest.

The closer they got to where the cattle were, the more Talmadge steamed. Rustling was bad enough, but killing livestock and leaving them laying was on a whole different level. He didn't know when or how, but Talmadge had it settled in his mind that those men would pay for what they'd done.

Sure enough, upon further investigation, there were 14 cattle lying dead at the bottom of the ravine, all wearing the Barkhouse brand. When he could calm himself enough to speak, Talmadge uttered only one sentence.

"Milo's got one chance to do the right thing."

That was all he said. He just eased back up in the saddle and rode off in the direction they'd come from. The boys glanced around at each other and followed suit. They'd never seen their father like this, and although Lake and Asa were grown men, it scared them.

*\*\**

That same evening, Talmadge rode into town to speak his piece to Milo.

Jasper Maxwell was sitting in a chair on the porch of the jail taking in the view when he arrived.

"Well howdy Talmadge," he said facetiously.

Talmadge didn't even seem to acknowledge his as he slid off of his horse and handed him the reins.

"Hold these," he commanded, never breaking stride as he walked across the porch and entered the jail.

The bewildered Maxwell looked down at the reins in his hand and up at Talmadge, but he didn't bother to stand. Talmadge left the door open upon entering and Jasper listened intently to his every word.

As he entered the room, Milo and Warren Clement sprung to their feet.

"W...wha....what's this all about?" Milo stammered as Talmadge came almost nose to nose with him.

"Your brother will be brought up on rustling charges and you're gonna do it," he told him matter-of-factly.

"Who says?" Milo fired back, finding his confidence.

Clement just stood in shock.

"I say," Talmadge replied. "It's bad enough to steal a man's cattle, but to kill them is a whole different thing. They drove 14 head off a bluff into a ravine. And they didn't even bother to cover their tracks this time!"

Milo tried to respond, but he was cut off.

"You've got one week to make this right," Talmadge said with a finger in his face.

Quickly, Talmadge turned on his heels and walked out the door.

"Talmadge, wait!" Milo called after him to no avail.

The door had already been slammed between them. Talmadge walked swiftly across the porch and fetched his reins from Maxwell, who still sat where he'd been left. Without ever stepping off the porch, Talmadge was back in the saddle in a flash. Having heard the intense exchange of words, several people had come out into the street from nearby buildings and watched as Talmadge rode easily back out of town.

# Chapter Seven

The next couple of days brought a great deal of worry for Talmadge. He couldn't believe he'd marched into the jail and demanded that Milo arrest his brother. It wasn't like him. Not that he didn't think he was right, he knew he was. It just wasn't like him to be so forceful; it never had been. But then again, he couldn't recall a time when he'd ever been this angry either. What Murphy had done had lit a fire in the patriarch of the Barkhouse family. It was anyone's guess now just who that fire would burn.

Belle was just as surprised, if not more so, by her husband's behavior when he told her what he'd done.

"What if you'd been shot?" she'd asked him.

"I don't know," was all he could muster at that point.

While she wasn't pleased with how Talmadge had gone about the situation, she didn't dare question his decision. That just wasn't something she did. Still, she worried, and with good reason.

Once he'd told the boys about his outburst in town, Talmadge knew there was one more person he needed to tell; his best and oldest friend Giles Kayser. If things were going to play out how he figured they would, he'd need all the help he could get and Giles was the best option he had. To be sure Giles would have his back; Talmadge thought enough of him to give his only daughter to one of his sons in marriage. Claire was now a Kayser and that made them family even if 25 years of friendship didn't.

\*\*\*

When Giles saw Talmadge crest the last hill before where the Kayser ranch laid, he knew exactly why he was there. Claire and Luke had been over for supper at the

Barkhouses' the night before when Talmadge announced the news. Luke had already talked to his father and his mind had been made up.

Talmadge's shoulders held the weight of the world as he approached. He didn't even offer a hello as he left his saddle and Giles didn't expect him to.

"You talked to Luke?" he asked.

Giles nodded his head as he led his old friend over to a couple of chairs that sat near his corral. They both took a seat and watched as a new, unbroken pony wandered around its enclosure.

"What do you think?" Talmadge asked.

Giles seemed to be mulling it over, but he didn't turn his attention away from his new horse. His friend's silence bothered Talmadge. He kept casting quick glances over at him, but when he got nothing, he too turned his attention to the horse, hoping it had the answers he so desperately needed.

When Giles finally did speak, it wasn't exactly what Talmadge wanted to hear.

"It weren't smart, Tal."

"Oh, I'm well aware of that. I'm in over my head now."

"Sure enough."

Talmadge wasn't feeling any better about his situation and all Giles would do is stare at that pony prancing back and forth.

"Gonna start breaking her tomorrow. She's off of good stock, but they all got a wild streak in 'em," Giles noted.

Talmadge could feel anger beginning to wash over him. All he needed was a vote of support from a familiar face and the man he came to for it was no help at all.

"You remember that old bay mare I had with the white rump?" Giles continued. "Probably had it 15 years or so ago."

Giles looked over to get Talmadge's answer.

"Yea," he mumbled, annoyed.

"Same blood," Giles told him as he pointed to the pony.

Giles knew Talmadge wanted more from him, but he needed to let it simmer a bit before he told him how he felt. He knew it took time for Talmadge to become angered and in light of his latest actions, he was curious as to whether he was still dealing with the same man he'd known for so long.

"What I'm sayin' is," Giles said. "We go back a long ways. You're the closest thing I've ever had to a brother. We fought tooth and nail side-by-side for better than three years in a war and however many since."

"But...," Talmadge pushed, sensing the tone of Giles' voice.

"I've got to do what's best for my family."

Talmadge stood quickly from his seat and looked down at Giles with an intense look of both astonishment and rage.

"You just said I was your brother!"

"I said you were the closest thing I had to a brother, not blood," Giles retorted as he too stood to his feet. "That's my family. They've got my blood running through their veins," he added as he motioned toward the house where his family was.

"What about Claire?" Talmadge asked harshly.

"She's married in, she's family. I'll look after her like I will my own. I told you that when she married Luke."

"And you think I took it lightly giving her to him in marriage?"

"No, I don't," Giles replied. "I know it had a good deal to do with our friendship; and I don't take that lightly."

All Talmadge could do was stand with his hands on his hips and shake his head in disgust. He just couldn't believe that Giles didn't have his back on this.

"You of all people," he said. "I thought I could count on you when I couldn't turn to anybody else."

"He's gonna kill you. You know that don't you?" Giles asked. "You've kicked a hornet's nest and now they're gonna sting."

"And I'll take my lumps when they do. But I'll do it like a man."

This remark set Giles over the edge. He couldn't take such a comment without rebuttal, even from a friend.

"You need to leave," Giles said as he stepped up closer to Talmadge. "You brought this on your own family."

"I'll remember this."

Talmadge wasted no time mounting his horse. As he left, he turned back to face Giles and hurled one more remark at him.

"It ain't just gonna be me. When I'm dead and gone, you just wait and see how long he lets you operate!"

As Talmadge made his way back home, his countenance was heavy. He was angry, of course, but more than anything he was sad. He felt as if he'd just lost his only hope of possibly evening the odds with Murphy Cole. To be turned away by a man he'd been in battle with hurt. He had no idea what he'd do next other than fight for his life.

***

Unbeknownst to Talmadge or Giles, two of their sons were about to make a decision that would speed along the process of Murphy Cole's wrath.

Asa Barkhouse was Talmadge and Belle's second oldest son, and even though he was born just days after Luke Kayser, he'd always been close with the younger Simon. They were the wildest of the 11 boys the two families had in total. None of the Barkhouse or Kayser boys were ever into any real trouble, but these two were definitely the most rambunctious of the bunch. At 23 and 20 respectively, they believed it was their place to do something about Murphy Cole.

Asa's father had flown off the handle, but hadn't taken any measures to get the upper hand and Simon's father didn't want anything to do with the conflict at all. Asa and Simon planned to act in the exact opposite manner.

The morning after their fathers had met, the boys set westward toward the outskirts of the Cole ranch after a secret meeting the night before. With neither of them having any pressing work at hand, they headed out together from the Barkhouse home, a practice not uncommon for them. Although he wasn't pleased to see them leaving with such heavy anticipation in the air, Talmadge's only condition for them leaving was that they go armed. With what they had in mind, this was a request they were more than willing to fulfill.

After riding due north for a ways to avert any suspicion, they cut southwest and hit a creek bed they knew would carry them within a half a mile of where they wanted to be without ever breaking trail. With both of the boys having a strong command of the terrain that held the three cattle ranching operations around Langston, their ride was an easy one. They'd barely worked their way up onto level ground when some of Cole's cattle came into view.

"We need to get to high ground, see what's around," Asa noted.

They came to a stop and Simon retrieved his father's army-issued telescoping looking glass from his saddlebag to have a gander. Glassing around, he spotted a slight hill with a small stand of oaks on it to their right.

"That hill yonder's our best bet I reckon," he told Asa, pointing out the spot.

"Alright. We'll ease back down the creek bed and around. Don't want 'em seeing us, but I wanna get there soon."

Knowing each other well, the two young men set out for their new destination. About 30 minutes or so of careful riding put them where they wanted to be. After hitching their horses to a couple of oaks in the stand of trees they'd seen previously, they crawled up to where the hill crested with just their guns and the spotting glass.

Asa had an old, heavy Colt Dragoon his father had given him when he turned 16 and a borrowed double barrel shotgun. Simon had brought along a Colt Paterson and an 1860 Henry rifle. All four weapons were loaded to the hilt, and though neither of the young men had seen combat before, they were willing and ready if the need were to arise.

While willingness is a virtue common among youth, patience is not. Fortunately, both Asa and Simon had been raised to be patient. It took some time to come to fruition, but finally, in the afternoon, their patience was rewarded.

"Asa," Simon whispered, nudging his friend who laid beside him on his belly.

Asa turned his attention toward what Simon was studying with the looking glass.

"There they come."

"Let me take a look."

Simon handed the glass over to Asa, who took his time surveying the area. Below them, several hundred yards out was a group of men on horseback gathering small groups of the cattle that wandered about on the plain.

"Six of 'em," Asa said as he tried to determine just who they were.

"Best I could tell."

As the men worked their way closer, he began to be able to pick some of them out.

"Looks like Preston for sure out front... Maybe Hildebrand."

Dallas Hildebrand was probably Preston Cole's best friend as he was one of only a couple of his father's men who were near his age. Hildebrand was either 19 or 20 depending on what story you believed, but he definitely had at least two bodies to his name. In all actuality, he was the only one in Cole's outfit that anyone outside of their crew knew for sure had killed a man. Suspicions of pretty much all of the men were aplenty, but there was nothing confirmed of the others.

One of the men turned toward them, allowing Asa to take a good luck at his face.

"That's Lewis turned this way," he remarked, referring to Adam Lewis, the youngest and most hotheaded of the crew.

What they didn't know was that Lewis had seen them too.

"We've got company," he told Jeremiah Cook, the younger brother of Gene, Murphy's first-in-command.

"Where?"

"Up on that hill to the north. Don't look too hard. There's two of 'em."

Jeremiah took a brief look for himself, acting as if he was inspecting a couple of the furthest cows. The six men mingled about, sneaking quick glances up at their observers. They came together in a wad with their backs mostly turned toward Asa and Simon as if they were oblivious to their presence.

"You think they know we're here?" Asa asked Simon, who now had the looking glass.

"If they do, they're doing a fine job of acting like they don't."

Once again, Asa took a look and seemed satisfied with his friend's assessment.

"Any idea who it is?" Gene asked the group.

He was in his 50s now and his eyes weren't nearly as sharp as they had been in years past. He now had to rely on the vision of his younger cohorts.

"Probably some of the Barkhouses," Adam said.

"It don't seem like a Talmadge play though," Preston added.

"No it don't," Gene agreed.

"Who's to know with him now? With the way he acted in town…" Phillip Clark, another of Cole's men.

Clark was in his 30s and had always been a cowpuncher as long as he'd been working. He'd proven his worth with a gun to Murphy though in their retreat north from Texas. No one among the group doubted whether he'd step up in the event of a gunfight.

"Very true," Gene told Phillip.

"It's your call Gene, you know that," Preston said.

As far as he was concerned, his father had the utmost confidence in Gene Cook and that was good enough for him. Gene had been with Murphy about as long as Preston had been alive and Preston had never seen his father question the man's decisions about anything. In fact, Jeremiah had joined the crew some six or seven years ago without so much as Murphy knowing anything other than the fact that he was Gene's kid brother.

"We're gonna spread out and round up these cattle; push 'em back toward home," Gene started. "We'll circle back if they follow and go from there. I don't want to call for no unnecessary killing without your pa's blessing."

Gene looked to Preston to gauge his reaction to this decision. Preston just nodded in agreement, his faith in the man unwavering.

"You heard the man," Preston told the crew. "Let's spread out."

Asa and Simon watched as their plan was set in motion. Simon was a bit concerned with this meeting of the minds they had just watched, but Asa seemed unbothered by it. It didn't take long for the six men to have the cattle gathered and heading toward home. Gene rode lead with Preston bringing up the rear and the other four spread out through the herd. They closely watched the herd and crew as they headed out of sight, waiting to make their move.

"You still think we'll be able to get some of their cows without getting too close?" Simon asked.

He was becoming less and less confident in their plan to take back some of the cattle that had been stolen at the orders of Murphy Cole.

"Oh, we're fine," Asa said assuredly. "I'm sure they didn't push 'em far. Just didn't want 'em getting too far out of pocket.

If he was worried, Asa didn't show it in the least. Simon wanted to be as positive as his buddy, but it just wasn't happening. Still, he wasn't going to let Asa go it alone. So when they were sure they couldn't be seen and had eaten the last of their provisions they had brought with them, they went back to their horses and saddled up.

They went back the same way they'd gotten to the hill and down into the creek bed where they knew they were less apt to be seen. Upon reaching the end of the creek bed where they had surfaced previously, they spotted some cattle to their left that hadn't been their earlier.

"Probably the ones they pushed back earlier," Asa noted.

The pair looked about carefully, and when they didn't see anyone, began to round up a couple of dozen cattle. This wouldn't replace all the cattle that had been taken or killed from the Barkhouses, but Asa knew it was a start. They were almost ready to go when Simon noticed that his horse had gone on full alert, his ears pricked up high and puffs of air blowing out of his nose.

Simon took a look around to see what his horse was noticing. The hair stood on end on the back of his neck when he saw Adam Lewis and Phillip Clark trotting right at them on horseback. It was as if they'd appeared out of thin air.

"Uh, Asa," Simon stammered.

Asa looked to his friend to see what the matter was. Simon couldn't speak, he only nodded in the direction of the approaching riders. They were scarcely a hundred yards away when Asa laid eyes on them.

"Shit," he muttered half under his breath.

Before their minds could even begin to fathom a plan to escape their predicament, the boys heard more approaching hooves.

Whipping their horses around quickly, they spotted the rest of the crew they'd been watching earlier closing in on them. By now, Adam and Phillip had come to a stop within ten paces of the frightened young men. Phillip's rifle laid across his saddle, hammer cocked, and Adam had his hand laying eagerly on the butt of his revolver.

The eight of them sat on their horses in deafening silence: Asa and Simon couldn't speak and Cole's men wouldn't. They only smiled their devious smiles as if this was all just a game to them. Truth be told, it probably was.

Just when they thought their ear drums would explode from the pounding of their own hearts, Asa and Simon caught the sound of another approaching horse. Looking left, they saw who it was. The sinking sun in the western sky made him hard to see clearly, but there was no doubting who it was cutting that daunting shadow: Murphy Cole.

"Well, well, well," Murphy started with a sneer. "What do we have here?"

"Looks an awful lot like rustling to me, sir," Preston answered enthusiastically.

"I'd say you're right son."

Murphy reached in his shirt pocket and retrieved a cigar and match. He struck the match across his saddle and lit his cigar, puffing it a little to get the fire going. When it was ignited to his liking, he tossed the match aside and took a long draw from the cigar, inhaling it slowly and exhaling it through his nose before looking closely at Asa and Simon.

"You boys realize rustling is a hanging offense, don't you?" he asked.

Neither of them could bring themselves to speak.

"That is what's going on here ain't it?" he continued.

"We were just taking back some of what you took from us," Asa replied shakily.

"And just what did I take?" Murphy asked wryly.

"Cattle," he said as he dropped his head.

Murphy let out a great, deep belly laugh and pulled on his cigar once again. His men also laughed among themselves at the fear in Asa's voice. The only thing funnier to them was the fact that Simon Kayser was here scared to death when he had no skin in the game.

"Just where'd you get the idea that I took your cattle?"

"My pa."

"And where'd he get that idea from?"

Asa knew that it was Black Curtis that had told Talmadge who'd done the rustling, but he also knew that revealing that information would more than likely cost Curtis his life. He was already here without his father's knowledge or approval; he couldn't very well risk the life of a good man as well.

"I don't know," he lied.

"That's alright," Murphy told him. "I know."

Asa snapped his head toward Murphy, curious as to whether or not he really knew. If he did, did that mean Curtis was dead? Probably so, he figured.

"And now I know that you know," Murphy said. "It's okay though."

Asa almost let himself relax a little at this answer, but Simon was almost in tears. He knew they were in dire straits. Murphy just let them squirm while he continued to calmly smoke that cigar. Finally, after more than a minute of agonizing silence, he spoke.

"Take 'em home boys," he said as if it was to no one in particular.

The meaning of this command was lost on Asa at first, but Simon knew what it meant immediately. He went for his pistol, deciding that if he was going to die, he was going to do his best to take someone out with him.

From there it was over in a flash. Phillip leveled his rifle and shot Simon in the chest and right off of his horse. Simon fumbled for his gun momentarily, but that was brought to a halt quickly as Gene Cook planted a finishing shot in his chest as well.

Asa's hand had barely even made it to his gun when he was slammed in the back of the head by a bullet from Adam's pistol. He slumped over in the saddle motionless, only falling when his horse bolted from beneath him. And just like that, it was over.

Murphy smiled as he looked down at the carnage, before taking a draw from his cigar and heading home.

***

As dusk fell, Talmadge was ready to come unhinged. He couldn't believe those boys weren't home by now. Belle busied herself with preparing supper to avoid thinking the worst. It didn't work though; she was a bundle of nerves as well. Talmadge sat at the table, doing everything he could not to explode.

"Where on earth could they be?" he exclaimed, startling Belle.

He'd done this without thinking.

"I'm sorry," he said quickly.

She couldn't tell if he was angry or scared, or both. Truth be told, it was a great deal of both. Most of his anger, though, was aimed at himself. How could he have just let them go out alone? Who knew where they were now, or where they'd been all day for that matter?

"I'm sure they're fine," Belle said, but she didn't believe it. "You know those two. They probably got all caught up funning about."

Talmadge wanted to agree with her sentiment, but he knew inside that neither of them believed it in the least.

"Maybe you're right."

Try as he might, he couldn't wait any longer so he went to the front door and hollered out.

"Lake!"

In a matter of moments, his eldest son came around from the back of the house where he'd been fiddling with some woodwork, his hobby of choice. He knew by the tone of his father's voice, though, that his attention was required immediately.

"Yes sir?" he asked.

"I want you to ride out to the Kaysers' and see if they've heard or seen from Asa or Simon," he instructed. "I'd go myself, but Lord knows Giles don't wanna see my face."

"Yes sir," he replied, turning to go get his horse.

Talmadge stopped him though.

"Carry a gun, son."

Lake nodded as he walked over to the wall where several of the family's guns hung. He grabbed his gun belt as Talmadge looked on. He swung it around his waist to buckle it when he stopped in his tracks. His father looked at him curiously.

"What is it son?"

Lake held a finger to his own lips and cocked his right ear in the air. Talmadge and Belle did the same, listening intently.

"A horse," Lake said softly.

Sure enough, Talmadge and Belle began to hear it too. A single horse was approaching at a fast pace. Maybe it was Asa, realizing he was in a whole heap of trouble for worrying them half to death. Just then, one of the boys' panicked voices rang out from the yard.

"Pa! Pa!"

Suddenly, two shots rang out and smacked the outside wall of the house.

"Belle, get down!" Talmadge screamed as he rushed toward the wall to grab a gun.

She hit the floor in a hurry as her husband had demanded. Taken aback a bit, Lake froze momentarily. He snapped out of it and snatched the pistol out of its holster and headed for the door with his father hot on his heels with a rifle.

By the time they got outside, the rider was too far to shoot, heading east at breakneck speed. Augustus came around the house to their right and joined them. He'd had the best look at everything that had happened.

"It was Adam Lewis!" he said excitedly. "He was dragging him behind his horse!"

Talmadge's head snapped around as he looked fiercely at his son.

"He was dragging who?!"

"Asa," he replied as he diminished to tears.

He pointed over at his brother's body lying motionless on the ground about 15 feet from the house. In their haste, Talmadge and Lake hadn't even noticed him. Talmadge ran over and hit his knees beside his dead son. His head spun as he took in the grisly site. The back of Asa's head was demolished from the bullet that had been planted there.

Turning him over on his back wasn't much better. His face was disfigured as well and he'd obviously been dragged for quite a distance over harsh terrain. A rope was tied snugly around his ankles and the end had been cut, relieving the horse of its burdensome load.

"Talmadge!" Belle yelled out.

He turned and saw her running over from toward the house.

"Get her back in the house! She don't need to see this!" he barked at the boys.

They tried their best to restrain her, but it was to no avail. She forced her way past them and hit the ground beside her husband. Her chest heaved as tears streamed down her face, but she felt as if no air was reaching her lungs. She just cradled her son's ruined head and cried silently.

The rest of the boys gathered around, hugging each other and crying. Talmadge just sat back on his heels and stared off into space. He couldn't cry, he couldn't speak; he could only stare. For once in his life he felt like he had no idea what to do next.

He knew this thing between him and Murphy Cole might get ugly, but he never could have guessed it would come to this.

# Chapter Eight

News of the previous day's events was delivered to Montgomery Cole early the next morning. He'd been awake a while, studying his Bible in preparation for his upcoming sermon. With a bit of studying and prayer behind him, he headed out to the café to have breakfast, an almost daily ritual for him. Just as he shut the church door behind him and began down the front steps, one of his congregation members and a friend of the Barkhouses and Kaysers, Tom Walton, called out to him.

"Preacher!"

The preacher whipped his head around to the right in the direction of the nearby railroad tracks to see who it was that was addressing him. Upon seeing Tom, a great wide smile came across his face. He was always happy to see one of his church faithful, and Tom seemed quite excited to see him as well.

"Oh, good morning, Tom! How are you? Won't you come have breakfast with me?" Monty asked happily.

Tom was in a hurry, closing the distance between the two of them at a quick pace. Monty seemed to notice this, but didn't particularly think much of it.

"Preacher, have you heard?" Tom asked eagerly.

He thought that was a bit vague, but perhaps Tom was just having a little fun with him.

"Have I heard what?" he asked.

"About the Kayser and Barkhouse boys."

This piqued his interest. As far as he knew, nothing had happened with the two families as of late. He did know that there had been some cattle stolen from the Barkhouses, supposedly by his brother, but he didn't know for sure if it was true. It wouldn't surprise him if it was though. Perhaps this was related to that. Whatever it was, he wasn't sure he was going to like what he was about to hear.

"What happened?"

"Asa Barkhouse and Simon Kayser are dead," Tom said solemnly. "Your brother and his men killed them."

This was definitely not something that he was prepared to hear. His face held no expression as he tried to process this information he'd just been given. Sensing that the pastor was struggling to come to grips with what he'd told him, Tom spoke again.

"He accused them of rustling."

Now this he just couldn't believe. Had his brother and his men rustled some of the Barkhouses' cattle? Probably so. But had Talmadge stolen some of Murphy's in return? No, there was just no way.

"Who knows about this?" Monty asked Tom.

"Most everybody I suppose," he answered. "Whole town's talking about it."

"Oh."

He stood there contemplating what he should do. Tom just waited patiently to see if there was any way he could help.

"I guess I need to go see them," he said.

"You want me to ride out with you?" Tom offered.

Monty shook his head slightly.

"No, I'd better go alone."

"Alright then. You know where to find me if you need me."

To tell the truth, Tom was relieved that his company wasn't requested. He considered both Talmadge and Giles friends and brothers in Christ, but it was a great deal of sadness to be around.. He didn't for one moment envy the position that the reverend currently found himself in.

Monty's stomach was in knots. It was all he could do to force his feet to take him back inside the church. He trudged across the porch and inside to the back, where his living quarters were. There he hit his knees beside his bed and prayed.

"Dear Heavenly Father," he said aloud. "A great evil has fell upon us here. You know Lord that we spoke about this and I asked if it be your will, that this would pass us by. I see now Lord that this is not your will."

He paused momentarily as he struggled to choke back the tears that were trying their best to escape from his eyes.

"Help me Lord to do what is in accordance with your will regardless of my personal feelings. Show me the way Lord and I will follow it. I am your servant. Amen."

He opened his eyes and forced himself up off his knees and into action. He grabbed his Bible and saddle blanket and walked out the back door.

Not wanting to face the townspeople before he had a chance to go speak with the grieving families, he slipped along the backside of the buildings as much as possible down to the livery stable that sat at the end of the street at the far end of town. Luckily, no one stopped him to chat, and the few that did see him only waved in passing.

Upon his arrival there, he was met by Lyle, the stable keeper. Monty didn't own a horse of his own, but Lyle was a member of his church and always had one for loan anytime he needed it.

"Well howdy there, preacher," Lyle said cheerfully.

Monty had figured that Lyle hadn't heard about the death of the boys and this basically confirmed what he'd believed.

"Good morning, Lyle," he returned.

Lyle's kindheartedness was a bright spot that he desperately needed considering the task that he had before him. It wasn't that Lyle was a simple man because he wasn't. He was just hard-working and preferred to spend his time with animals rather than in the company of other people. Taking care of something that needed his help appealed to him much more than being caught up on the town gossip.

"You're going for a ride I see," he remarked, taking notice of the preacher's saddle blanket.

The preacher looked down at the blanket in his hand, nodded, and then raised it up as if showing it to him.

"Oh, yes. If you've got a horse I could take out for a bit."

"Always," Lyle replied. "Over here."

Monty followed Lyle over to a stall where a young bay mare stood calmly. She nuzzled up to Lyle's neck as he patted hers. The preacher reached up and stroked her muzzle, a gesture which she seemed to appreciate.

"She's a friendly thing," he remarked.

"Best horse I got," Lyle said. "Small, but gentle as they come."

Monty studied the horse, her behavior never changing. She reminded him a great deal of one his father had owned when he was a boy. It was just as gentle in demeanor and almost identical in appearance. It made him long for simpler times, times when he wasn't in the middle of what was becoming a blood feud between his brother and men he considered friends. Life growing up had been hard, but this had the makings of possibly being harder.

That horse hated Murphy and he was beginning to share that sentiment. He knew it was wrong to feel that way, especially about his kin, but most of the difficulties he had ever experienced in life had been related to his brother in one way or another. Suddenly, it was as if he wasn't even standing in the stables. Physically he was, but his mind wandered. Lyle's voice broke his trance.

"So you wanna take her out?"

He'd been watching the preacher and could tell he was distracted so he gave him a moment to gather himself.

"Uh, yea," Monty replied once he'd come back around to reality.

Monty stepped out of the way as Lyle swung the stall door open to led the horse out.

"Come on, gal," he said to her softly.

Without a hitch, she followed him over to a half-wall where several saddles were lined up waiting to be used.

"You saddle her so she knows you're in charge," Lyle instructed.

The pastor did as he was told, gently spreading his saddle blanket across her back and strapping on one of the saddles. He reached over to the nearby wall and fetched a bridle which he slipped over her muzzle and buckled it into place. Throughout this whole process, she never budged or resisted. Lyle had been exactly right; she was as gentle as any horse he'd ever had dealings with. He rarely had the need for a horse, but he knew which one he'd be riding when he did.

Once he'd finished preparing the mare for riding, he turned to Lyle.

"What do I owe you?" he asked.

Lyle just shook his head.

"As long as you're doing the Lord's work, you don't owe me a dime."

"Well I'm doing my best."

Lyle smiled and shook the preacher's hand.

"Keep her as long as you need her. I know she's in good hands."

"Thank you much," Monty replied as he stepped up onto the horse and settled into the saddle.

As he rode away, Lyle simply turned back to his work. The preacher led the horse around the livery and started out. He'd go north to the Barkhouses', the further of the two ranches first, then head east to the Kaysers' on his way back to town. All along his way, he prayed quietly to himself.

Upon his arrival at the Barkhouse home, Montgomery was immediately met by two overwhelming emotions that overtook the family: sorrow and anger. Belle was doing all she could to stay busy while Talmadge begged her just to be still and calm. This was not something she could do though. Her time to grieve the loss of her son would come, but right now she needed to stay as busy as possible to avoid that.

"Let me get you some coffee, preacher," she pleaded. "Won't you have something to eat?"

"Oh no, I'm fine," he replied. "I'm here to serve you, not the other way around."

"I insist," she told him.

He began to protest again, but a quick glance shared with Talmadge told him that it was better just to go along with her insistence. Talmadge had reached the point that he knew there was no sense in trying to force her to rest. This was her way of dealing with this whole ugly ordeal.

"Well, alright," Monty told Belle. "But just a little something."

He took a seat at the table with Talmadge as they waited to be served. The preacher scarcely had an idea of what to say to either of them. Although he felt he had the Lord on his side, there just didn't seem to be any words that could do justice in this situation. It was his brother, after all, that was to blame for their son being dead in the first place. He was thankful that a beautiful breakfast of steak and eggs was set in front of them before the conversation had ventured much beyond small talk.

"Thank you much Belle. This looks delicious," he bragged. "Won't you join us and have some?"

She hesitated. He looked at her, trying to figure out a way to convince her to take a break.

"It'd sure make me happy to have breakfast with you. I'll even serve you," he said as he stood.

He didn't give her a chance to balk at this idea, knowing that playing on her desire to please people left her with no other choice but to give in. She took a seat as the preacher took a plate from the cupboard and fixed her a healthy ration. He placed it in front of her before grabbing a cup and pouring it full of coffee for her.

"There we go."

Belle and Talmadge both smiled as Monty took his seat. This meant a great deal to them both, especially Talmadge, who was grateful that someone could get her to be still. She probably hadn't been in one place for more than 10 minutes since Asa's body had been dragged up. She was already exhausted and he hadn't even been dead a day.

After saying grace, the three of them began to eat.

"Sure is good, Belle," the preacher remarked as he took a sip of his coffee.

"I'm glad you're enjoying it," she said solemnly.

She barely picked at her food, but Monty seemed to genuinely enjoy it. He scarfed down the steak and eggs as if it was the best thing he'd ever eaten. It was definitely better than his usual breakfast of whatever was being served at the café in town. Not that it wasn't good, but they just didn't have the touch like Belle's home cooking.

As he ate, the pastor noticed that Talmadge wasn't eating much of his food either. He was typically a ferocious eater, so it was quite obvious that he was in a state of disarray. Belle laid her fork down and dropped her head over into her right hand. Tears welled up in her eyes as she rubbed at her temples.

"I think I might lie down for a while," she said suddenly.

Both men stood as she excused herself to their bedroom.

"I'm sorry, preacher," she said through tears as she left the room.

"Don't you worry about that," he assured her.

He and Talmadge sat back down to their breakfast. As relieved as he was that Belle was finally trying to rest, Talmadge was just as concerned that she was beginning to break down. With her out of sight, his mind turned more toward the contempt he held for Murphy Cole rather than his grief at losing his son. As Monty was finishing off his coffee, Talmadge couldn't hold himself back any longer.

"There weren't no rustling going on," he said sharply.

This caught the preacher off guard. Once he'd registered what Talmadge had said, he could tell where this conversation was going.

"Is that what they said?"

"Walton and Jefferies rode out here this morning to check on us. Said they heard that some of your brother's men were in the saloon bragging last night."

This was definitely news to Monty. He'd been at the café last night before heading back to the church for bed and nobody had said a word.

"First I've heard of that."

"Who told you?" Talmadge asked.

"Tom Walton stopped me on my way out of the church and told me.

"He sure made it back to town in a hurry," Talmadge noted.

"Yea, I suppose he did," Monty said. "He said word was all over town."

Talmadge was wondering about the preacher's story. He really didn't doubt anything he told him, but right now his wariness was at an all-time high.

"You seen your brother?" Talmadge asked.

"Sure haven't."

"That bastard killed my boy. And one of the Kaysers too. I'll see him hang or rot in Hell."

This was bold, harsh talk, especially in the presence of clergy, but he was past the point of caring. Although he couldn't condone the behavior of his friend, Monty could certainly sympathize with it. He wasn't a father himself, and didn't figure to ever be, but he'd conducted the funerals of a few children and young people who had gone before their parents and it was never easy. All of those had been as a result of accidents or sickness, but this was far different.

"I understand, Talmadge, but you can't let your anger cloud your judgment right now," he said unconvincingly.

This was not at all what Talmadge wanted to hear.

"With all due respect preacher, this ain't your job. I got a lot of respect for you, but I need you to preach my son's funeral and console my family. As for what happens next, you leave that up to me."

Monty had been in the ministry long enough to realize when he needed to back away. As much as he wanted to help Talmadge, he understood that he was in a dark place at the present moment. This was uncharted territory for the Barkhouses and a set of circumstances that one was not likely to ever completely recover from.

"Okay," Monty said. "When will the funeral be?"

"We'd like to have it tomorrow at two," Talmadge answered.

"Alright. I've got to go see the Kaysers about Simon, then I'll let you know."

"It'll be at the same time," he told the preacher. "They'll be buried in the same place. We've had the plot picked out for a while. Us and them."

Monty noticed that Talmadge was beginning to choke up as he thought about the fact that he'd be burying one of his children the next day.

"I just never thought I'd be burying a youngin', especially not like this," he said through stifled tears.

Neither man knew exactly what to say so Monty just placed a reassuring hand on his friend's shoulder. It was a simple gesture, but it did not go unnoticed by its recipient. At this point, all Monty knew to do was to pray and be there when needed.

"I reckon I'd better go," Monty said. "I've got to get over to Giles' place. You just send word if you need me."

"Will do," Talmadge replied. "We appreciate it."

In just a matter of moments, Talmadge had gone from a bitter, vengeful man and back to his typical self. Monty knew that Talmadge was a good man who loved God, he just hoped that side of him would be the side to prevail.

The two men rose to their feet and Talmadge saw his guest off as he rode away from one distraught home to another.

***

Upon his arrival at the Kayser home place, Monty found a situation that was both similar and different from the one he had just left behind at the Barkhouses'. What lacked here was the anger. Instead, there was just a deep, brooding sadness that hung over the whole landscape.

In much the same way that Asa's body had been delivered home, so had Simon's. Phillip Clark was Murphy Cole's messenger that was sent to the Kaysers'. Unlike Talmadge, Giles hadn't made some magnificent act of grandeur in the sheriff's office challenging the Coles. In fact, he hadn't done anything at all. The only Kayser that was guilty of doing anything at all out of the way was Simon, and all he'd done was be a loyal friend to Asa. Unfortunately for him, it had cost him his life.

Giles met the preacher outside so as not to disturb Judith, their girls, and Claire who were inside. It was just him and the ladies there at home. Luke and Daniel were out with the Barkhouse boys, cutting wood and building caskets for their brothers.

"I just can't believe it preacher," Giles said.

"It's a difficult thing, I know."

Giles turned to Monty with a look of disgust on his face.

"This all happened because of Talmadge, you know. He was all Hellfire and brimstone, gonna take down Murphy Cole. Didn't he know these boys would be listening to that?"

His voice was filled with animosity. Monty wanted to deescalate the situation, but he knew deep down that there was at least a little truth in the accusations made against Talmadge. However, the blame here laid with his own brother and he told Giles just that.

"I understand," he said. "But you can't blame Talmadge here. My brother started this. I reckon he just thought he was doing what was best."

Giles knew that Monty was right and trying to keep the peace between him and his oldest friend, but he was hurting. One of his sons was dead and all he could do was hurt. Right now Talmadge was an easy target. He'd acted out of character and it had eventually cost Simon his life; but it had also caused Asa's death as well. He wanted to hate Talmadge, or Murphy, or somebody, but right now he didn't have room for anything in his heart for anything but pain. Suddenly he burst into tears.

"I'm sorry," he said as he tried to stop himself from crying.

Monty took a step closer and placed a hand on his shoulder.

"Don't worry about it brother," he told him gently. "Matthew 5:4 tells us 'blessed are they that mourn: for they shall be comforted'."

Although he was a religious man, Giles was not thrilled to hear what the pastor had to say. In times like these, it was difficult to see the light at the end of this tunnel that appeared to be never-ending. The sentiment and effort were appreciated on the outer surface, but hard to accept on a deeper level.

When Giles had had some time to gather himself, Monty spoke up.

"Talmadge tells me y'all will be burying the boys in the same grounds."

Giles only nodded.

"Does two o'clock tomorrow work for the service?"

"That what Talmadge said?" Giles asked.

"Yea," he said softly.

Giles seemed to be thinking it over as Monty awaited an answer.

"That'll be fine I reckon," he answered unconvincingly.

Monty could tell that there was more than a shred of uncertainty in this answer so he gave Giles a moment to think it over.

"We can do it another time if you'd rather."

"No. We need to be as cordial as we can be," he said as he shook his head.

"Whatever you want, Giles," the preacher said. "Is there anything else I can do?"

"No, I reckon not," Giles replied.

"Well, you'll be in my prayers. All of you. And I'll see you tomorrow unless you call on me before then."

The two shook hands as the preacher mounted his horse and pointed her back toward town. This ride back gave him time to think over the exchanges he'd just had with the two grieving fathers. There was a definite rift between the long time best friends, but now was not the time to feed that ugly beast of isolation. He knew that somehow he must try to help mend this bridge between the two. They were both good men, and the sooner they realized that they were on the same side of this issue, the better.

If there was one thing that Montgomery knew about his brother, it was that Murphy Cole was both relentless and ruthless.

# Chapter Nine

Asa Barkhouse and Simon Kayser's double funeral was held the next afternoon at two o'clock as planned, with Reverend Montgomery Cole officiating.

Their families had chosen a beautiful patch of land for which to bury them in in. Quite morbidly, choosing this shared family burial ground was one of the first things they had done when they settled their respective ranches.

What would become the Barkhouse- Kayser Cemetery was a flat meadow by a creek that ran almost the entirety of the two ranches from east to west toward the Powder River. Several large oak trees shaded the scenic area that sat virtually on the border between the lands belonging to each of the families. It was almost fatalistic that such a fitting final resting was positioned so conveniently for two families who had shared so much over the years.

The crowd that turned out for the event was respectable, but perhaps not as large as it might have been had it not been drizzling rain intermittently and the circumstances been different. While the representation of the townsfolk of Langston wasn't bad, there was no doubt that attending the funeral of a pair of alleged cattle rustlers potentially held a negative connotation. This was especially true when you considered the fact that their accuser was one Murphy Cole, a man who had no reason to fear repercussions from the local law due to the fact that this law was his next to kin. A man with such free will could almost do as he pleased, even to the point of becoming a tyrant.

Conversely, Murphy's brother Monty was doing all he could to be the guiding moral light of the community in the wake of these hideous happenings. He preached fiercely and prayed fervently as he eulogized these two boys who, along with their families, had been stalwarts in the church of Langston since their arrival as adolescents.

"I consider it a great honor," the preacher had said. "To commit these two fine young men back to your care Lord. Not many people, young or old, are cut from the same cloth as they were."

If Murphy Cole had pledged a great deal of effort into painting Asa and Simon as criminals, Montgomery had worked twice as hard to demonstrate to those present just the opposite. For what it was worth, Monty's description of them was considerably the more accurate of the two.

As for the families, they all wept. The fathers, mothers, sisters, and brothers. Every single one of them cried, whether quietly to themselves or sobbing uncontrollably. All except for one.

Several of the people in attendance noticed this, and made note to themselves, and perhaps to each other in private, but never publicly.

Augustus Barkhouse was the only member of either family with dry eyes. Rather, his eyes were ablaze with a raw fury that you could almost see consuming him from the inside out. He looked as if he could break out in a manic rage at just any moment. Since the day that he'd watched his brother be dragged up to their house dead, he'd been different. He'd looked into the laughing eyes of Adam Lewis as he cut Asa's dead body loose from his horse and it had changed him. He would remain this way for as long as he would live.

When the service was over, most of the crowd was quick to extend their brief condolences and leave for home. Tom Walton and his wife, as well as Herman Jefferies and his wife were the last people left besides the families and the preacher. Tom and Herman filled the graves of the boys so that their own kin wouldn't have to do such a depressing chore themselves. This gesture was greatly appreciated by both parties.

The ladies, Sharon Walton and Esther Jefferies, also offered to cook them a meal, but both families were exhausted so they politely declined.

"Are you sure there's nothing we can do?" Herman asked.

"No," Giles said. "You've done more than enough."

"And we appreciate it greatly," Talmadge added.

With nothing left to do, the Waltons and Jefferies left the grave site and headed back home.

The women and girls boarded their buggies and the sons mounted their horses in preparation to leave while Talmadge pulled Giles aside for a brief word.

"We've got to go to the sheriff," Talmadge said, his voice hushed.

Giles just looked at him with a half smirk on his face.

"And why would we do that?"

"They murdered our sons, Giles."

Talmadge couldn't believe that he was actually having to explain this. How could Giles not be outraged? Simon was just as dead as Asa, and at the same hands.

"You really think it's gonna matter?" Giles asked. "Murphy's justified it as rustling, and even if he hadn't, do you really think there's anything that Milo would do? That's his brother!"

Although the two men were speaking quietly, there was an intensity in their conversation that told their families that it was less than friendly. Everyone was on edge.

"Well, we've got to do something," Talmadge continued.

"Like it or not, our hands are tied, Talmadge."

Talmadge thought of how he'd found out that it was Murphy was responsible for his cattle going missing in the first place.

"Maybe not," he wondered aloud.

This response and how he'd said it as if he was half talking to himself intrigued Giles.

"What do you mean?"

"What if we could get somebody to testify that it was Murphy and his men who rustled my cattle first? To be sure a lawyer could build a case off that."

Giles agreed that this plan seemed plausible, but he had no idea how they'd pull it off.

"But who's gonna witness?" he asked. "You know Murphy's men are too loyal, or scared, or both to buck him."

"Black Curtis," was all Talmadge said.

"Curtis?" Giles asked confusedly.

"That's how I found out it was Murphy stole my cattle."

"He told you? When?"

Talmadge recounted his story to Giles.

"When I rode out to Murphy's the week they went missing, Curtis caught up with me on my way back. Said he'd overheard them talking about it and thought I should know."

Giles took this information in and pondered it. He wondered if it would work and even if it would work, would Curtis be willing to stand in a court of law and point the finger at Murphy Cole? A man would have to be mighty bold to do such a thing.

"We couldn't go to anybody local," Talmadge continued. "It'd be too easy for Cole to get his hands on 'em."

"Maybe Miles City," Giles suggested.

"Maybe," Talmadge nodded.

"Would they take the word of a black man though?" Giles asked.

"Out here, I believe we'd be alright," Talmadge assured him.

Talmadge kept saying "we", and Giles desperately wanted to be a part of that "we", but he had a hard time believing they'd ever be able to stop Murphy Cole. Especially with such a thrown-together plan.

"Look, Giles," Talmadge said. "I don't want nobody else to die no more than you do. I just want justice for these boys. Murphy Cole aims to have what I own and probably what you own after that. He can't do that in jail or at the end of a rope."

"We'll talk more," Giles said. "I need to get them home."

"Alright then."

They shook hands, then led their families back to their respective homes. Although they'd both just buried sons, Talmadge and Giles both couldn't help but feel a little relieved. They were coming back around to one another. Perhaps, on the same page, they had a chance.

***

"Heard you preached them boys' funeral," a familiar voice said to Montgomery Cole.

The preacher looked up from his supper of ham and beans into the eyes of his brother Murphy. His other brothers Milo, Marvin, and Melvin stood just behind Murphy, sneering. They always seemed to have some sort of look of supreme confidence about them whenever they were behind him.

Monty sat at a table in the café that was tucked back in one corner where he typically ate his meals. It was quiet and to itself, but he remained approachable if anyone should need or want to speak to him. From here, he could see pretty much the whole room and door. He'd seen his brothers enter, but chose not to address them until they came to him.

"I sure did," he answered his brother.

Murphy took a seat at his table directly across from him and the others joined him. He reached over and grabbed Monty's spoon he'd laid down. He took it and scooped himself a big bite of Monty's food. He grunted as he chewed and swallowed it.

"Hmm, not bad," he remarked.

"Here, have some more," Monty said, annoyed, as he slid what was remaining in the bowl over to Murphy.

"Don't mind if I do."

He took the bowl and ate the rest of the ham and beans that were left in the bowl. Monty looked on as he did so, but none of the five of them said anything. Really, he had nothing he cared to say, and he knew the others wouldn't speak before Murphy led them in. Murphy's play here was not lost on Monty; it only served to further the distaste that was growing inside him toward his brother.

The few other people who were also having their supper tried to act as if they didn't notice the meeting of Coles in the corner, but it was painfully obvious that they did. Though he was generally a quiet and private man, Murphy did love for people to see him in charge, so this added attention was more than welcomed by him.

As he scraped the bowl clean, he set the spoon back in it and slid it over to Monty's side of the table.

"Thanks, brother."

He grabbed Monty's glass of water and washed down his food with it before wiping his mouth with Monty's napkin. All of this was done deliberately as his brother looked on in silence. When he was done, Murphy sat back in his chair and stared over at Monty. He studied his neatly pressed black shirt, the white clerical collar just marking a difference in color at his neck. He noticed Monty's clean-shaven face and finely combed hair. Monty wasn't like him or his brothers; he never had been. One thing that they did have in common though, was a growing resentment for one another.

"You ought not to have done that, you know," Murphy finally said.

Monty just stared back for a moment.

"What's that?" he asked dryly.

"You know exactly what I mean."

"Apparently I don't," Monty fired back.

Murphy let out a short laugh, but there wasn't an ounce of actual amusement. He looked over to Milo.

"You wanna tell him?"

Milo's face lit up. His number had been called and it was his time to shine. He, Marvin, and Melvin all lived to please Murphy, but his position as sheriff afforded him the opportunity to be of extra help to the cause.

"Them boys was rustlers," he said matter-of-factly.

"Says who?" Monty snapped back.

Regardless of what they might think, Montgomery Cole was not scared of any of his brothers in the least. His retort had caused Milo to stumble a bit. He looked to Murphy, then answered Monty with as much confidence as he could muster.

"I do. I am the sheriff after all."

"So they stood trial? I heard nothing of it."

Monty was hitting back just as quickly as Milo could come up with another volley. Murphy looked uncomfortable. His idiot brother was getting taken the best of.

"No need for trial," Milo sputtered. "They went for their guns."

"Oh, so you were there?"

"Well, uh, no."

He was fumbling harder for words and Murphy was squirming.

"Then who told you?" Monty pushed on.

"I did," Murphy interrupted.

"So your word is gospel now?"

"On this matter, you bet your ass it is."

Having Murphy speak up on his side gave Milo the confidence to sling another barb at Monty as well.

"If you think about it, they really had no choice in the matter," he said.

"It that right?" Monty asked.

"That's right," Milo and Murphy said in unison.

All four of the opposing brothers smiled as if they'd just won some great battle. Monty gave them no indication to the contrary. He just sat there quietly as if he was soaking in his defeat. Along with what Milo and Murphy had said, he also heard everything that Murphy hadn't said.

"If you've got something you want to say to me, you can just say it," Monty said coolly.

Murphy snickered a bit.

"I'm not saying anything," he told him. "Just mind who you associate with... brother."

With that said, he stood to his feet and instructed the other three to follow suit.

"Let's go."

As they left, it was as if all of the air was seeping back into the room. No particularly harsh words had been spoken, nor had voices been raised, but the atmosphere was almost vibrating with tension. The few people who had remained during the exchange began to slip out of the door. The preacher tried to keep up a brave face, but he was ashamed to have been party to such a conversation, especially in public, and especially with family. Fear was a strong word, but it began to creep into Monty's mind.

# Chapter Ten

Giles Kayser was another worried man. He'd been a nervous wreck ever since Talmadge accosted Milo in the jail, but it had only gotten worse since Simon and Asa had been killed. He had never been fearful, but he was always cautious. For the first time in as long as he could remember, Giles was genuinely worried.

You'd always find Giles on the side of who and what he thought was right, but up until now, that had never jeopardized the health and well-being of his family. He'd not even been worried like this when he left home to fight in the war. He knew he was raising good boys and had a strong wife. His life had been the only one on the line then. This time was different.

He'd now seen firsthand what Murphy Cole was capable of and it scared him. Like Talmadge, he'd never been a great admirer of the man, but he never expected this to happen either. Neither one of them could guess that such an intense darkness brooded inside that man. While he could appear to be just another fella, he was far from that in reality. They had no idea the kinds of things he'd done in the past or what he would do in the future without the slightest hint of remorse.

They: Giles and Talmadge. For years, they'd basically been a cohesive unit. It had been just shy of 19 years that they had known each other. Giles had moved his family from his native Virginia, up into West Virginia, and across the Tug Fork into Kentucky; just a few years before the blood feud between the Hatfields and McCoys had erupted. Giles had no idea that he would be on his way to a possible blood feud of his own a couple of decades later.

Further into Kentucky the Kaysers pushed until they settled in the quiet town of Twin Forks where they met the Barkhouses. Judith and Belle were fast friends, with Giles and Talmadge being a bit slower to take to one another. When they did become friends, it was a bond that couldn't be torn asunder. It had been tested when the Civil War broke out and Kentucky claimed neutrality and the country seemed to be collapsing around them.

When fighting became inevitable, they chose to stick together. The two of them fought side-by-side proudly and kept each other alive. When the conflict was over, it was a combined decision between the two families to do something they had little to no experience in. Within six months of Giles' and Talmadge's permanent arrivals back in Twin Forks, they headed to Arkansas to gather a herd of cattle, which they drove northwest together.

Upon their finding of Langston and settlement nearby, they split the cattle evenly into two separate herds. The decision to keep two separate ranches was made to keep things simpler whenever the patriarchs passed on. Having too many heirs laying claim to the same estate would undoubtedly lead to problems, especially with 12 children eventually being had between the two families. Although the families had remained close over the years, no one could know what could possibly happen in the future. This current situation was a shining example of just that.

The more that Giles mulled over his past with Talmadge, the more convinced he was becoming that he should help out his old friend. He could honestly say that any time that conflict had risen during their friendship, Talmadge had never backed down from a fight. Whether it be the war, Indians, or any other obstacles that had come up along the way to Langston or since they'd been settled, he knew he could rely on Talmadge. His willingness to fight had allowed them many years of peace until just recently.

However, it had been quite some time since they had been involved in any fighting and the years of hard work had taken their toll on Giles' body. Tending to cattle was enough work in itself without the thought of fighting of a war with Murphy Cole that seemed to be hopelessly futile. Not that Giles was helpless, but he figured that a conflict such as this would have to be fought largely by his sons, and that was a price he wasn't sure he was willing to pay.

So here he found himself stuck between what he thought was right and what he thought was wise.

His doubts were not lost on his family. Judith could tell. Daniel and Luke could tell. Even Mary and Martha, who were just 9 and 6 respectively, could tell. The weight of this situation fell heavily on them all and they all had their own unique opinions of what should and should not be done.

Giles knew that his daughters heard much of what had been said in the household and he wished that his decision was as simple as the way it seemed in their minds. 'Doing the right thing' and 'being a good friend' were such easy things to say in theory, but much more difficult to do in practice. Being a father and husband that his family could respect and admire was important, but even more important was being alive to be there for them.

It was with this thought that he made up his mind just what he would do.

\*\*\*

"I'm scared," Claire Kayser told her husband Luke as they sat down to eat their supper.

This abrupt proclamation caught Luke off guard. Claire wasn't one to worry, much less share her feelings aloud in such a manner.

"What about?" he asked.

"This whole mess with Murphy Cole," she said softly.

"Oh honey, that's gonna be just fine," he told her, knowing he was likely lying.

Suddenly, she burst into tears and hid her face in her hands. Luke jumped up from his seat and went over to comfort her.

"Oh darlin'," he whispered as he bent over her and wrapped his arms around her shoulders.

This scared him. Claire was a lot like her mother. She was resilient and strong showings of emotion didn't just happen without a great deal of suppressed feelings of some sort.

"It's gonna be okay," he said, half trying to convince himself.

He knew just as well as everyone else did that this was far from over. Blood had been spilled and it wouldn't be the last.

Claire stood to her feet and turned herself into Luke's embrace. Her knees wavered and she would have fallen if not for him supporting her weight. All she could do was sob. Her body heaved as she tried to take in air and tears poured from her eyes like the rains of a summer thunderstorm, but she didn't make a sound.

She'd never been this scared before. Even when they were on their way north to what they now called home, she wasn't this terrified. She was younger then and looked at Talmadge and Giles as invincible and capable of taking on any challengers, and they had been. This was different though. Claire was older and saw Talmadge for the absolutely vulnerable human he was. She also saw Giles as such, and she wasn't even sure he was going to back her father as they had done for each other so many times before.

Luke just held onto his wife, not knowing what to say and wondering what she would say. It seemed like hours that they stood there wrapped up in each other. Their little house that sat between the Barkhouse and Kayser ranches felt as if it was states away from anybody. Right now it was just two people who had known and loved each other their whole lives alone in their own little world. Things would obviously never be the same. They'd both lost brothers and stood a chance to lose more loved ones so they just held onto each other.

# Chapter Eleven

Talmadge avoided Langston as much as he possibly could in the wake of Asa and Simon being murdered. As much as he desired retribution, he was hesitant to put his family at risk in order to seek it. He knew that any unnecessary trip into town could put him and his family in the line of fire for Murphy Cole and his men.

The time had come that a trip had to be made though. Almost the entire family's clothes were threadbare and the lighter material needed to make new ones for the upcoming warmer weather was lacking at home. On top of that, most of their horses needed new shoes, and while Talmadge and the boys could shoe them themselves, they needed to see the blacksmith to have the new shoes forged.

Early in the week, Talmadge sent Lake into town alone to place the order for the horseshoes. He'd managed to slip in and out of town without seeing or being seen by any of Cole's men. Now though, it was time to retrieve their order and material for their new clothes. Because Belle needed to be there to figure how much sewing supplies would be needed, Talmadge decided to make this trip to town into a family affair. They'd hardly gone to church since Asa's death, and when they did, the socializing was kept to a minimum. Murphy Cole had been there with a smile on his face on each of those occasions. He made it abundantly clear that he would not hide.

When the Barkhouses prepared to go into town, Talmadge left Lake at home to watch over things. Orel asked to stay and his parents obliged. He'd become even more reclusive since Asa had been killed and they felt that some alone time with his favorite brother may do him some good. Besides, there really needed to be more than one of them at the house to keep an eye out.

"Any trouble comes up and you can, send Orel into town to get me," Talmadge instructed Lake.

"Will do," Lake replied.

"You hear me, son?" he asked Orel.

"Yes sir," he said softly.

"Alright then. We'll be back as soon as we can."

So away they went; Talmadge and Belle on the buckboard with Avery, Augustus, and Chauncey following behind on horseback.

***

The family's trip to the blacksmith went off without a hitch. Jip, the weathered, gray old proprietor of the shop had all of the items prepared on time and of the highest quality.

"Fine work as always, Jip," Talmadge remarked.

"Thank you," Jip said. "I don't make good product, I don't eat."

"Fair enough," Talmadge smiled. "The money Lake brought you enough?"

"Yep. We're square."

Talmadge extended his hand out and Jip shook it.

"Thank you again."

Jip nodded and Talmadge turned to go back to Belle and the boys. He stopped just shy of the door and turned back to face Jip.

"If you don't mind, don't say nothing about us being in town. I know folks are bound to see us, but I don't want to make a big fuss about it. We're gonna get what we need and head home"

"I understand," Jip assured him. "I won't say a word."

Talmadge tipped his hat in thanks and left the shop.

Jip's shop was just inside the end of town furthest from the railroad tracks, near the livery stable and easy to access discretely. In order to purchase the material they would need for clothes, they must travel further into the heart of town. Luckily for them, their friend Tom Walton's wife ran a shop that carried materials such as these, allowing them to avoid Marvin Cole's store. The selection wasn't quite as varied, but it was more than adequate to meet their needs, especially given their tumultuous relationship with the Coles.

Belle selected items to purchase and handed them to Talmadge to carry while Avery attempted to flirt with the Waltons' niece who had recently come to stay with them. Augustus and Chauncey stood outside by the wagon in waiting.

The town was moderately busy, but most of that action was taking place closer to the middle intersection of roads. All of the Barkhouses were glad of that fact. This meant that they could quickly handle their business and be gone before anything could be made of their presence in Langston. For now, they needed to be as far away from the Coles and any of their friends and associates as they could realistically be. They weren't running or hiding, but it was a wise thing to do. Perhaps if they stayed away enough, some sense of normalcy may eventually return.

Few people in town really believed that Asa and Simon had been doing any cattle rustling, but they found themselves in an awkward position nonetheless. If what Murphy Cole said was true, then he was in the right. Maybe he'd gone about it the wrong way, but the fate of the boys was still the same.

And if it wasn't true, Murphy Cole had the money and the manpower to instill fear in people. Throw in the fact that his brother was the law in the town and its surrounding areas, he was virtually untouchable. He'd never done any killing here before, but his first foray into it had been bold.

That left the Barkhouses in the predicament they were in, shying away from the town they had called home for so long. They'd all seen or heard about Talmadge's outburst at the jail. It was at the very least provocative, a verbal finger-poke in the chest meant to evoke a response.

Things for the Kaysers were much different. They hadn't openly challenged Murphy Cole in a town it appeared that he was now in control of. Simon's death was considered a sort of 'wrong place, wrong time' issue, even by Murphy himself. This close association with the Barkhouses was viewed as the only thing that they had done wrong. Up until now, that had been only been considered a positive relationship. Things in Langston were changing though.

Belle and Talmadge were almost finished with finding the needed supplies and preparing to checkout. Thankfully for them, there had been no other customers around and they were moving about at a quick pace. Outside though, tensions were about to rise.

Augustus and Chauncey were waiting quietly when two familiar faces appeared down the street. Augustus recognized them as soon as they exited Melvin's saloon and walked out into the street. Chauncey didn't seem to be paying them any attention, but Augustus was on full alert. His outlook on their situation differed greatly from the rest of the family. Despite their sadness and anger of Asa's death, they had pretty much resigned the fact that they were in over their heads in trying to go toe-to-toe with Murphy Cole. Taking him on was just asking for more blood to be shed.

Bloodshed was exactly what Augustus wanted though. He couldn't overlook his brother's death or the possibility of losing more. All he knew was that Adam

Lewis had dragged his dead brother into their yard and he was now in his sight for the first time since that day.

Clark and Lewis turned down the sidewalk and began walking toward them, down the same side of the street as the Waltons' store. Augustus glanced down into the buckboard where the guns they had brought with them laid. They hadn't worn guns on their persons, but they were not naïve enough to go into town completely unarmed.

They drew closer as Augustus watched and Chauncey remained oblivious to their presence. When they were about 20 paces away, they appeared to notice the Barkhouse brothers. They stopped on the boardwalk and seemed to be talking something over. A devilish grin spread across Adam Lewis' face as he locked eyes with Augustus. This time though, Augustus' eyes didn't hold surprise or fear, they were filled with raging hate and bloodthirst.

Adam stepped out into the street to walk across and Phillip followed suit. As they made their break, Augustus snatched the shotgun from under a blanket in the buckboard and jogged at an angle across the street, circling around in front of his targets.

Chauncey snapped out of his mindless daze as he saw his brother quickly leave him. Upon seeing the shotgun in Augustus' hands, he knew that trouble was to come.

"Gus!" he yelled as he leapt out into the street to run after him.

Augustus paid him no mind, but a few others took notice, including both of Cole's men. It was too late though. Without them even realizing it, Augustus had gotten across the street in front of them. Lewis looked in the direction of Chauncey's voice, but didn't find Augustus.

Augustus watched as Lewis quickly scanned the street before calling out his name.

"Adam Lewis!"

Adam turned and saw Augustus but it was too late. The shotgun was at his shoulder and he emptied the left barrel into Adam's chest with a bang. They were less than 10 feet apart so the whole load of buckshot found its mark. Adam melted in a heap and Phillip Clark froze in place. Augustus took a couple of steps forward and took aim at Clark. Click! The second shell didn't fire. Augustus was caught off guard momentarily, but came back around when he saw Clark's hand go for his pistol. He quickly stepped forward and slammed the butt of the shotgun into Clark's chin, knocking him out cold.

"My God!" Chauncey exclaimed as he ran up to where the bodies laid.

Augustus finally noticed his brother, but he was almost in a trance. He'd done what he'd wanted to do and now he was basically numb. Chauncey snapped him out of it by snatching the shotgun from him.

"You need to go!" he demanded, pointing in the direction of their horses. "Get on your horse and ride!"

He shoved Augustus toward the front of the Waltons' store and followed behind him.

Inside the store, Talmadge and Belle had been paying for their goods when they heard the shot. Immediately, they knew something had happened with the boys. Talmadge dropped what he had in his hands and sprinted for the door. As he hit the porch, Augustus was swinging up into his saddle. He charged away out of town as Chauncey arrived and threw the shotgun into the wagon.

Talmadge looked over to where Adam and Phillip laid out and people were gathered around, then back to Chauncey.

"What did you do?!" he screamed.

"It wasn't me," Chauncey told him. "We need to get out of here though."

Chauncey quickly mounted up and rode away as Belle and Avery exited the store.

"Get aboard!" Talmadge commanded Belle. "On your horse!" he told Avery.

"What's going on?" Belle asked.

"I'll tell you on the way. Just get aboard!"

Belle and Avery did as they were told and Talmadge forced the wagon forward, heading away from Langston as quickly as possible.

\*\*\*

Lake and Orel were out behind the house straightening some things up when they heard the rumbling of someone approaching on horseback.

"Do you hear that?" Lake asked, turning to Orel.

Orel nodded and they broke toward the house where they had a rifle and pistol lying in wait. Lake grabbed the rifle and levered a bullet into the chamber while Orel retrieved and cocked the pistol. The horse's footsteps grew louder as they went around either side of the house to see just who was coming. They both were on edge and had their guns aimed and ready to fire.

Much to their relief, it was Augustus who was returning home. But why was he in such a great hurry and where were the others? As soon as he could see his younger brother's face, Lake could tell that something was terribly amiss.

"What's wrong?" he asked excitedly. "Where's everybody else?"

Augustus skidded the horse to a stop. They were both out of breath from their furious ride.

"They're on the way," Augustus replied. "I've killed Adam Lewis in town."

"What in the hell were you thinking?!" Orel snapped.

Both Augustus and Lake turned their heads quickly to look at their baby brother. It was highly uncharacteristic for him to speak with such passion and language.

Augustus slowly dismounted and looked over to Orel, his head down a bit, seemingly in shame.

"I weren't thinking, I reckon," he said.

All three of them looked back toward town as their parents and other brothers could be seen coming toward home. Orel looked over at Augustus in disgust and came over to his horse.

"Give me the reins," he ordered. "I'll put him away."

Augustus did as he was told without any rebuttal. His head was already in a whirlwind and he didn't know what to make of Orel's sudden change in behavior.

Orel took the stud away to clean up, feed, water, and put up for rest. Augustus and Lake stood in silence as they waited to see what would happen next. Truth be told, neither of them knew what to say.

As soon as Talmadge could bring the buckboard to a stop, his feet were on the ground and he was in Augustus' face. Augustus was the second oldest of the living boys and just as big if not slightly bigger than his father, but he felt like a small child as Talmadge's eyes pierced his.

"Have you lost your mind?" Talmadge asked, enraged.

Augustus didn't know what to say, if anything at all. He couldn't tell if this question was rhetorical so he stayed quiet. Apparently it wasn't.

A vicious backhand took Augustus to a knee.

"Talmadge!" Belle shrieked, but it fell on deaf ears.

Augustus stood and another hard backhand put him back where he had just come from. He looked up at his father with tears rolling from his eyes and blood pouring from his mouth. It was not unusual for Talmadge to use his hand to discipline his children, but this time was different. That was out of love, this was out of rage. Augustus struggled up to his feet and Talmadge reared his hand back again. Before he could swing it this time though, Lake stepped between them and grasped his wrist.

Lake shook his head at Talmadge and forced his hand down. Everyone looked on in awe. It was unprecedented for one of them to defy their father, but they knew it was the right thing to do in this instance.

"That's enough," Lake told his father, his wrist still clenched.

Talmadge tried to pull his wrist free and Lake let him. The two stared at each other harshly before Lake spoke again.

"He did something stupid. Now we've got to fix it, not make it worse."

Talmadge stood in disbelief, still staring at Lake. He looked around at the others and began to see that his son was right. When he looked at Augustus, he nearly cried himself. Gus' face was already swollen around his mouth and stained with blood. His eyes were bloodshot and his head pounded from the concussion of the blows.

Talmadge's face softened and Lake stepped aside to allow him to reach Gus. He wrapped his battered son in a tight hug and choked back tears.

"I'm sorry, son," he sniffled.

"It's alright, Pa," Augustus told him.

They let go of the hug and Talmadge held him at arm's length as he thought.

"They'll be coming for you," Talmadge said. "We'll have to see if the Kaysers will keep you."

Belle still sat on the buckboard. She had been too afraid to move during the whole encounter.

"Get on the buckboard and I'll take you over there. I don't want to leave your horse there in case Milo and his men check there."

Belle climbed down so they could board. She was in tears as she embraced Augustus. She touched softly at his injured face and wiped as much of the blood away with her kerchief as she could. Talmadge was aboard and waiting with the reins in his hands.

"We've got to go now."

She kissed his undamaged cheek and hugged him once more before letting him go. She really didn't know if she'd ever see him alive again. Giles and the Kaysers hadn't been too keen on getting involved anyway and she didn't believe they'd be quick to harbor a fugitive. It was their only hope though.

She leaned on Avery and Lake as they watched them ride east, out toward the Kayser ranch.

***

When Talmadge and Augustus arrived at the Kaysers', the greeting they received was less than warm. And this was before they'd even told them why they were there.

Giles knew that something was wrong when he saw the two of them approaching. It had been ingrained into his mind lately that anytime he saw Talmadge, it only brought more trouble to him and his family. This time was no different.

As Talmadge quickly explained what brought about their hasty visit, a strange feeling began to develop inside of Giles. He didn't know exactly what it was. It wasn't exactly anger or grief, or even a combination of the two, but Giles knew it was not a feeling that he enjoyed. He did know, however, that it was likely one that he would continue to feel for quite some time.

"I told you I couldn't get involved," he told Talmadge sternly.

"I know," Talmadge replied. "And I wouldn't be here if I had any other choice."

Talmadge and the rest of the Barkhouses had always been likable people and not without friends, but this was something you couldn't take to just any friend. This left him at the mercy of his oldest and dearest friend.

"I know what you said, Giles," he continued. "But I need you. We need you."

He put his hand on Gus' shoulder as he spoke. Gus had great big tears welling up in eyes doing their best not to fall. Giles tried to avoid eye contact with him so as not to be swayed by emotion.

"I don't know," Giles said uncertainly.

His desire to steer clear of this conflict with Murphy Cole was subsiding and Talmadge could feel it. He knew that what he was saying was beginning to work.

"You've got to know, Giles," he told him. "You've got to know because I've got to know. I hate to put you on the spot, but they're gonna be coming for him and I've got to protect him. He's my boy. He did a foolish thing, but he's my boy and he did it with the right intentions."

Giles toed nervously at the ground with his boot, afraid to commit to an answer.

"Look," Talmadge told him. "I know why you're scared. Frankly, I'm scared too. But we've spilled blood before. Some of our own even. Now, we've already got a dead son apiece, don't let me have two."

Talmadge could tell that Giles was nearly broken down now. He didn't have much time though, so he needed one final blow to bring that wall between them down.

"I didn't want to go there, Giles, but I'm going to. I've had seven children, but only one little girl. And I gave her to your son. You know what kind of trust that takes? I value her life as much or more than any man walking God's green earth."

That did it. Giles understood the bond between a father and his daughter. After all, he had two of them. Even though they were very young, he knew that he wouldn't just hand them over to anyone in marriage when that time came. He also knew that Talmadge took that decision with Claire just as seriously and that Luke was lucky to have her.

"If I do this, that makes me all in, in their eyes," he told Talmadge. "They find out I had something to do with this and they'll be coming after me and mine too."

"And I won't forget who helped me when nobody else could," Talmadge assured him.

The two men shook hands, forging an agreement that had already been sealed in blood. Talmadge hugged Augustus tightly, not really knowing if it would be the last time he'd have a chance to do so. He felt remorse for hitting him like he had, but he was doing what he could to make up for it.

He climbed up onto the buckboard and looked down at Giles and Augustus.

"Get him someplace safe and don't tell me where," he told Giles. "If I don't know, they can't find out. I've got to get back."

He tipped his hat and rode homeward.

\*\*\*

Lake went out to greet Sheriff Milo and his deputies upon their arrival at the Barkhouse home due to the fact that Talmadge had yet to return from the Kaysers.

"Howdy, Lake," Milo said in greeting.

"Sheriff."

Milo and his men glanced around, trying to determine just what they had ridden into.

"Can I help you, Sheriff?" Lake asked with a hint of sarcasm in his voice.

"Where's everybody else? Your pa in particular."

"Don't know. He came back from town and dropped Ma off. Left here headed north not long after."

What the lawmen didn't know was that each of the Barkhouses inside was armed and ready. If the slightest thing went wrong, they'd all have lead flying their way. Lake himself had a small .32 tucked into his waistband at the back.

"What'd he do that for?" Milo asked.

"He didn't say. Probably checking in on the herd I reckon."

"And your brother?" the sheriff pushed forward.

A slight grin snuck across Lake's face.

"You'll have to be more specific sheriff. I've got five of 'em… well four now."

This rebuttal was not made in error. Lake knew exactly what he was doing. That barb was just enough to perturb Milo and let him know that his brother's actions weren't to be forgotten.

"Asa died as a result of his own actions," Milo struck back.

"So I've heard," Lake said coolly.

"This is different though," Milo informed him. "Adam Lewis didn't do anything wrong."

Lake allowed a look of surprise that actually appeared to be genuine to envelope his face. Milo noticed this and wondered if Lake really had been left in the dark concerning the events in town.

"Your brother killed him in Langston," Milo said, calling Lake's bluff.

Lake's eyebrows raised a little higher, but his response mirrored the facetiousness of those he'd previously offered.

"Specifics, Sheriff. Like I said, I've got four of 'em."

Milo couldn't make a read on Lake regardless of how hard he tried. His deputies were growing restless though.

"You know damn well which one!" Jasper Maxwell barked.

Lake looked him dead in the eye and responded.

"No… I don't."

As Milo was attempting to determine their next move, the familiar sound of a horse-drawn wagon coming closer became audible. All four men seemed to notice the sound at the same time. Upon turning their attention west, they saw Talmadge drawing closer in the buckboard. The four of them waited silently for him to reach them. He pulled the wagon up and climbed down, standing beside it and near Lake. A few logs laid in the back, covering up a rifle that was ready and waiting.

"Howdy Sheriff, deputies," Talmadge said with a tip of his hat.

"Enough with the pleasantries, Talmadge," Milo said coarsely. "Where you been?"

Talmadge acted as if he was surprised by Milo's unpleasant greeting, knowing full well he expected nothing less.

"Had to ride out and check on the herd, pick up a few old logs. Don't want 'em getting too close to your brother's place. Hate to cause more problems."

"It's a little late for that, don't ya think?" Roger Nelson cut in.

The Barkhouses studied these lawmen, trying to figure just how far this conversation was going to go.

"What are you getting at?" Talmadge asked.

"Where's Augustus?" Milo questioned.

"I don't know. Haven't seen him since we left town."

"Y'all rode out of there mighty fast from what I understand," Nelson said smugly.

Talmadge could feel the hairs beginning to stand on end on the back of his neck and a quick glance at Lake told him that he felt the same. Lake had fallen silent since Talmadge's arrival, allowing his father to do the talking. He was simply waiting for a clue as to what to do next.

"You boys got something on your mind, you should say it," Talmadge told them calmly.

Milo smiled a bit, annoyed by Talmadge's ability to act as if he was unbothered by this. Inside, Talmadge was a ball of nerves. He knew what Augustus had done was only further pushing the proverbial snowball downhill. From here, it could only gain speed and claim even more lives. Would those next victims meet their fate right here?

"Augustus killed Adam Lewis with a shotgun in town and damn near broke Phillip Clark's jaw," Milo retorted. "We're here to arrest him."

"Well as far as I know, he ain't here," Talmadge told them.

Finally, Milo stepped down off of his horse to be on level ground with the Barkhouses. His deputies followed suit. There they were, the six of them staring each other down with a palpable intensity. One side wanting information they knew the other one had, and the other side refusing to give up that information. Milo stepped up to look Talmadge eye-to-eye. Growing uncomfortable with the nonverbal message being sent toward his father, Lake took a couple of steps closer to the deputies.

"The rest of your family in there?" Milo asked Talmadge as he pointed to the house.

Talmadge only nodded.

"You better get 'em out here."

Talmadge mulled over his choices. He knew Belle and the other boys were likely armed inside, but he was more than an arm's length from his rifle with Milo standing right before him. If Milo was any shot at all, he'd have him dead before he ever got the rifle out of the wagon. He saw the pistol in Lake's waistband. He figured Lake could get one of the deputies, maybe two before they won the numbers game. From there, it was a crap shoot as to what may happen and he wasn't comfortable playing those odds.

"Belle!" he hollered out toward the house. "Belle, you and the boys get out here!"

"With your hands up!" Milo added.

The six of them waited anxiously to see if the remaining Barkhouses would come out in peace. Talmadge didn't think his boys would try anything crazy, especially with their mother in harm's way, but he was beginning to wonder just how much he knew about anything.

Momentarily, the front door eased open and Belle exited with her hands high in the air as she had been instructed. Slowly, the other boys came out behind her. Orel first, then Avery, and lastly, Chauncey. They all made their way over to Talmadge and Lake, where Talmadge wrapped his arm tightly around his wife.

"Now where's Augustus?" Milo asked no one in particular.

"We don't know," Belle said softly.

Milo took a quick, threatening step toward her, which was quickly met by Talmadge. He unwrapped his arm from around Belle's waist and stood between the two of them. Milo quickly halted, understanding the gravity of what his actions could lead to. Although they had the Barkhouses outgunned, he knew better than to go after the matriarch of the family.

"We're gonna check the house," Milo told them, turning his mind to a different task all together.

"Be my guest," Talmadge said.

"Fellas," Milo instructed. "Turn that house upside down. If that coward's in there, I want him out. I'll stay out here and keep an eye on them."

Augustus being called a coward angered the whole family, but there was nothing they could do about it at the present time. As the deputies disappeared into the house to execute their search, a dangerous thought entered Lake's mind. He considered snatching the pistol from his waistband and killing Milo. He knew he'd have the element of surprise and could put a bullet in Milo's head before he could get a shot off himself. He even went so far as to shift his right hand to his hip for quicker access.

Talmadge saw this move and suspected what Lake had in mind. He tried desperately to make eye contact with his son to instruct him not to do it. Lake purposefully ignored him though.

He knew it was the wrong thing to do so he crossed his arms across his chest and stood stock still. His father breathed an internal sigh of relief. Lake understood that killing Milo would mean the death of them all right there today. One five-shot .32 revolver and a rifle he wasn't even sure was in the wagon were no match for the guns of the three deputies. Perhaps they could grab Milo's pistol and guns from their horses, but that would take time they wouldn't have, even if the horses didn't spook. It would not have been a wise decision.

Inside, Nelson, Clement, and Maxwell did just as their boss had instructed them and completely ransacked the house. Not a single dish, utensil, cup, or anything of the sort was left in its place in the cupboard. Every bed was tossed and turned, including Talmadge and Belle's in the main bedroom. In the bedroom that the boys shared, their beds were torn apart and their clothes strewn all about. In Claire's old room, some of the things she had left behind when she married Luke were destroyed. They even stole a small roll of money that was tucked away under some personal items in a dresser.

After they were done with it, the house looked as if a tornado had blown through it. The deputies gathered up the guns that were in the house and brought them out to Milo.

"Awful lot of guns here, Sheriff," Warren Clement noted as they dumped them on the ground.

In all there were two lever rifles, a single-shot shotgun, and four revolvers. Milo grinned a devious grin as he looked down at this collection of firearms.

"What's one family need so many guns for?" Milo asked Talmadge.

"Protection."

Milo looked back down at the weapons and laughed to himself a little before turning his attention back to Talmadge.

"Y'all been doing something to need protection?" he asked mockingly.

"Nope," Talmadge replied. "We've lived hard lives that required the use of guns at times. In time, you acquire what it takes to get the job done."

"So you need 'em now, huh?"

"We hadn't in a long time. I guess your brother changed that."

Milo wasn't exactly expecting this answer and it showed on his face. He wasn't sure what to say because he knew that Talmadge was telling the truth. He pulled himself together though.

"We'll be taking these guns with us."

Talmadge wanted badly to give him a piece of his mind, but knew it was useless. Instead, he decided to be facetious himself as Milo and his deputies took their guns away and mounted their horses to leave.

"You don't want to check the barn?"

Milo grinned back at him and just shook his head.

"We'll get it next time 'cause we'll be back," he said. "I'm pretty sure Gus ain't here, but we're gonna find him and arrest him. And when we do, he's gonna hang."

Talmadge gritted his teeth to stop himself from saying anything else.

"Let's go, boys," Milo instructed his deputies.

As they rode away, Milo stuck his chest out as if he had accomplished some great feat. He hadn't retrieved Augustus, but he'd made a statement to the Barkhouses.

# Chapter Twelve

Talmadge and Giles met to discuss the next step to take the day after Milo and his deputies had paid their visit to the Barkhouses. They hadn't officially come to the Kaysers' to question them, but Luke had met Milo coming in that direction on his way into town. The men knew that Milo may have a hunch about Augustus' whereabouts due to the closeness of the families and that Augustus couldn't be left there long.

The two of them decided, after consulting with their families, that it was time to seek an attorney away from Langston. This would be their last hope at taking Murphy Cole down by use of the law. If that didn't work, they'd have to fight back any way possible, and they both knew that that would be bloody.

There was one man that Talmadge had to go see to determine whether or not this trip to Miles City was even worth taking. The only man who could tie Murphy Cole and his men to Asa and Simon's murders and the theft and killing of Barkhouse cattle: Black Curtis. There was no promise that this plan would even work, but for it to have a chance, Curtis had to be willing to testify against Murphy.

Talmadge had to be careful though. He had to find a way to reach out to Curtis without drawing suspicion. He knew of the weekly meetings that the Cole brothers held and that meant that the men who worked for Murphy were free to do as they pleased. For most of them, that meant heading into town to drink, gamble, or maybe find themselves a sporting lady.

Monty was the only Cole not invited to this meeting and Talmadge knew that. He had Luke go to Monty and asked him to have Curtis come in to do something for him while the meeting was going on. Monty didn't know whether or not his brother would allow him to come due to the tension between them because of this very relationship. He also didn't want to play part in anything that would lead to violence and was assured that this wouldn't happen. The preacher agreed to try.

In the church were several pews in need of some maintenance and Black Curtis could do anything. The church couldn't afford to hire a true carpenter, but allowing Murphy to help made him feel important and superior. In two days, when they were having their meeting and he had nothing else for Curtis to do, Murphy would send him to the church. When he got there, Talmadge would be there to ask him for a favor that would put them all at risk.

The time for the Coles' meeting had come and Black Curtis had been sent to the church to see how he could help Monty with those damaged pews. Upon his arrival, the preacher greeted him in a friendly manner.

"Good evening, Curtis."

Monty never called him by the "Black" moniker that most did, choosing to view him as a child of God rather than black or white.

"Your brother said you had some pews needed mending," Curtis said, setting down his box of tools.

"Uh, yeah," the pastor stammered.

Curtis looked around the dimly lit room, unable to really tell much about the pews and what work might actually need doing.

"To be honest preacher, I don't know how much I can do now," Curtis informed him. "I guess I can look around with a lantern to see what needs doing, but I'll need more light to work. Maybe tomorrow with the door open and the sun coming through the windows."

"That's fine, Curtis," Monty said. "But there's somebody here to see you."

Curtis' eyes grew wide with tenseness at this. He didn't know any reason that he should distrust Montgomery other than the fact that Murphy was his brother. Still, being brought here under false pretenses unnerved him.

Out of the shadows, Talmadge stepped forward.

"Howdy, Curtis."

"Oh, Talmadge," Curtis replied with a noticeable sense of relief in his voice.

Talmadge picked up immediately on this worry.

"Who'd you expected?" he asked with a laugh.

"I don't know," Curtis answered. "But I'm glad it's you."

They both shared a laugh as they shook hands.

"I'll excuse myself to my quarters," Montgomery interjected. "The less I know, the better."

Talmadge nodded as Monty excused himself. He pointed to a pew where Curtis took a seat across the aisle from him.

"What's this about, Talmadge?"

"I've got a mighty big favor to ask of you. No hard feelings if you can't or won't do it."

Many thoughts began to circle through Curtis' mind. He didn't know exactly what this favor Talmadge needed was, but he knew that it would somehow involve his boss.

"What's that?" Curtis asked.

Talmadge drew in a deep breath as he prepared to speak. He hated to even ask such a thing, but he knew this was his only possible hope at taking down Murphy without any further violence.

"If you can help me, I'm going to get an attorney, probably in Miles City, to try and take Murphy down," Talmadge informed him. "I want to do it without anybody else having to die if I can."

Curtis nodded intently.

"And what do you need from me?" he asked.

"If we've got a case, I'll need you to testify that Murphy was responsible for my cattle getting gone."

Talmadge figured that Curtis would balk at this request and waited with great anticipation. He didn't have to wait long though because he was given the answer he wanted soon after.

"I'll do it," Curtis said absolutely.

Talmadge's eyes widened and he sat straight up, surprised by the fact that Curtis was willing to help, especially answering him so quickly and certainly.

"Are you sure?"

He wanted it to be clear to Curtis what he could be risking by doing this for him and his family.

"I am," Curtis reassured him. "Ain't right, what he done. Especially killing them boys."

At this point, Talmadge knew that he had an ally and a reason to make that trip he had planned to Miles City.

"I appreciate it, Curtis. I'm gonna leave first thing in the morning and try to find a lawyer. I just need you to keep Murphy from finding out."

Curtis knew this wouldn't be up to him if Murphy had any reason to suspect that Talmadge was moving in that direction against him. He'd begun to show his true colors and Curtis wasn't sure where he would stop. Murphy had manpower and money, the two things that could take a man far in the world.

"You do what you need to do," Curtis told Talmadge. "But you'd better do it fast. He won't take Adam being killed lying down."

Talmadge knew he was right, he knew it all too well. He hoped he'd be able to set things in motion before Murphy struck again.

"I better go," Curtis said. "I'll come back and do this work tomorrow. Don't want Murphy suspicious."

He stood to go and Talmadge stood as well. They shook hands and Curtis left, grabbing his tools as he went.

Once he was gone, Talmadge went to let Montgomery know that their business was over.

"Thank you for setting this up," he told him as he came out of his room. "I just want this to be over. I can't lose any more of my kids."

"I understand," Monty replied. "I'll be in prayer."

"Thank you," he said again. "I need to get out of here. Got a long day ahead of me tomorrow."

The preacher nodded and they shook hands as Talmadge left, slipping out of town so as not to be seen by anyone who may be inclined to tell Murphy what they had seen. Tomorrow would be the beginning of a crucial few days that would decide just how much blood would be spilled before Murphy Cole was hopefully vanquished in one way or another.

***

The next morning, Talmadge saddled his and Augustus' horses early, packing enough provisions to get them to Miles City where they could restock.

After saying his goodbyes to Belle and the other boys, he headed for the Kaysers to retrieve Augustus. He needed a riding partner for the trip and getting Augustus away from Langston was a good idea for obvious reasons.

"This means more than you know," Talmadge told Giles while Augustus settled into his saddle and prepared for the ride ahead.

"Don't worry about it," Giles replied. "Just go get us some good news."

"I'll do my best."

He looked to Augustus to see that he was ready, and when he got the nod, they started out.

"Thank you, Mr. Kayser," Augustus said to Giles as they left.

Giles tipped his hat as he watched them ride north. He didn't have high hopes for their venture, but it had to be worth trying if it could help them avoid more bodies piling up. He was in the thick of this thing with Talmadge. Their personal losses were each other's now.

In their packs were a good amount of food and Talmadge had brought along his best suit of clothes to wear when he found a lawyer to help them with their case. Whether or not this tactic worked, he wanted to look his best when making the effort.

The two of them also wore six-shooters that Talmadge had retrieved from their small arsenal of weapons they had stashed in their barn. Thankfully for them, Milo hadn't called Talmadge's bluff on searching the barn when they'd been searching for Augustus.

***

Their two-day trip was uneventful, much to their relief. Upon their arrival in Miles City, they found a bustling place with more going on than they ever wanted. It didn't take long for them to miss the quaintness of Langston.

Their first order of business was to figure out where the attorneys in town had their offices set up. More important than that though, was finding one who could get the job done at a reasonable price. The two of them made arrangements to stay in a small boarding house for the night where they could have a bath and Talmadge could change into his good clothes. After some quick asking around, they believed they had found their man.

"I'm heading to the lawyer's office," Talmadge told Augustus. "If you happen to talk to anyone, introduce yourself as Avery. I don't know why any of that mess from home would have made it this far, but I'd rather play it safe."

"Yes sir."

Talmadge took a long look at his son and their room for the night before heading out. He didn't know whether this was worth doing, but he planned to find out.

After a short walk down Main Street, Talmadge found himself at the door of Isaac Mayock, Esq.

Inside, he found a neatly decorated, but simple office with one big oak desk arranged along the back wall. Behind that desk sat a round little man in a broadcloth suit, a thin mustache above his lip and sweat beaded up on his forehead. His thin black hair was also drenched.

"Hello there, sir! How may I assist you?" a shrill voice that didn't match its owner rang out to Talmadge.

Talmadge was beginning to regret this choice already without even hearing what legal advice he may offer. He didn't trust anyone that sweated so much without doing any manual labor. He even considered turning around and leaving without saying a word. Instead, he just stood there.

"Sir," the lawyer said, trying to snap him out of his apparent daze.

"Uh, yeah," he replied as he approached the desk. "You Mr. Mayock?"

A big grin swept across his face, turning his little mustache up on its ends.

"I most certainly am," he told Talmadge enthusiastically. "And you are?"

"Talmadge Barkhouse."

"And you're in need of legal advice," Mayock said knowingly.

"Yes sir," Talmadge nodded.

Mayock gestured toward a chair across from him and Talmadge sat down. He didn't know why, but he was actually starting to like this lawyer.

"How can I help you, Mr. Barkhouse?"

"I reckon I need to know your rate before we speak, Mr. Mayock."

The lawyer smiled widely and shook his head a little.

"Let's not worry about that," he told Talmadge. "You just tell me what's troubling you."

And he did. Talmadge told Mr. Mayock everything from his ever-present distrust for Murphy Cole, to his cattle going missing and being killed, to Asa's dead body being dragged up in their yard. He even told him up front that Augustus had killed Adam Lewis as retaliation.

Mayock sat there quietly, not once interrupting. He twisted his mustache and patted at his still sweating forehead with his soaked handkerchief, but not a word left his lips. In fact, he barely reacted to any of the information. For nearly an hour he sat in silence, until Talmadge brought up Curtis' willingness to testify against Cole.

"You've got a witness?" he asked, sitting forward. "And he'll testify?"

His excitement caused Talmadge to be a bit excited as well.

"Yes sir," he said. "There's just one thing."

"And what's that?"

"Well he's a negro, sir."

Mayock let out a big laugh, which caught Talmadge off guard.

"What's so funny?" he asked.

"We're not in Mississippi, Mr. Barkhouse. A black witness will be just fine."

Talmadge had to laugh a little at this response. For the first time since the first day they'd realized they had cattle missing, Talmadge was beginning to feel a little weight lifting off of his shoulders. He didn't want to get ahead of himself, but he couldn't help but enjoy this feeling.

"So what do we do next?" he asked his lawyer.

"I'll draw up the paperwork and talk to a judge. You just get the witness back as soon as you can."

Talmadge smiled, but the issue of payment still concerned him.

"What about money?" he asked.

"You pay me when we win this thing."

"Are you sure?"

"Not a dime before."

Mr. Mayock was confident and that confidence was starting to rub off on his client. Both men stood to shake hands and did so enthusiastically.

"I'll be seeing you soon, Mr. Barkhouse," Mayock said with a smile.

"You certainly will."

As he left and headed back to meet Augustus at the boarding house, Talmadge had an extra bounce in his step that probably hadn't been there in years. He couldn't help but feel as if the tide may be beginning to turn. He was cautiously optimistic, but the optimism was now outweighing the caution.

Unfortunately, back at home, the latest and greatest glitches in his plan were occurring.

# Chapter Thirteen

While Talmadge was handling his affairs in Miles City, Murphy Cole was about to do the same at home. It was about dusk and Murphy was in his normal evening spot: in his big chair in the den, admiring the mounted heads of several deer, elk, and antelope he had killed over the last few years in Montana. He was puffing on one of his big cigars, but did not have his usual glass of whiskey in his hand. Tonight, he wanted to be completely sober.

Curtis had prepared supper and all the men had eaten. They were free to do as they pleased for the time being. Some were in their rooms, others outside, and one still at the dinner table.

As Murphy half-enjoyed his cigar, Preston entered the front door and approached his father's chair. It took Murphy a moment to even realize that he was there. He was clearly distracted.

Preston looked down as if he was awaiting some sort of signal. Murphy nodded.

"It's time."

Without a moment's hesitation, Preston headed up the stairs to gather the men who were inside. Frank, Thomas, and Gene came down as Preston went out the back door to retrieve the others. Within a minute or two, all of Murphy's men except Curtis were assembled in the den. Murphy made them wait for a moment before he rose from his chair to face them.

"We've business to attend to in the barn, gentlemen" was all he said.

That was all he needed to say. They all knew exactly what he meant. Murphy led the way through the house and out back to the barn, which was situated directly behind the house about a hundred yards from the back door. They approached the barn with purpose, each step making a thud on the ground.

When they entered the barn, Murphy looked up to confirm that a lantern light was illuminating Curtis' bed up in the loft.

"Curtis!" Murphy called harshly. "Get down here. We need to talk."

Curtis knew by the tone of Murphy's voice and the amount of people he heard accompanying him, that this visit would not be friendly. He closed his Bible and looked over at his revolver. He considered coming out firing, but knew that there was a definite outcome with those actions.

"I'm not asking!" Murphy yelled up.

Curtis glanced at the gun again, but grabbed his lantern instead.

"Coming, boss!"

As he eased his way down the ladder, some of the others fanned out, hanging burning lanterns about to ensure that the barn was well-lit.

"What's going on?" Curtis asked as he climbed down.

When he reached the ground and turned to face Murphy, one look confirmed his suspicions that this would not end well for him. He wished now that he'd brought that pistol down with him. His fate would likely be the same, but he wouldn't go alone.

"You know what's going on, don't ya?" Murphy asked as he walked toward Curtis.

He was a good deal heavier than Curtis, but he held only an inch or two on him in height. Curtis wasn't intimidated by Murphy's size, but his intangible power was another story entirely. Still, Curtis did his best to maintain his composure.

"No, I don't," he told his boss confidently.

Murphy didn't smile. He wasn't in the mood for any cute games that Curtis may try to play. His cigar took the brunt of the punishment, being gnawed almost in two.

"Your little visit to see my brother the other night..." he trailed off.

"Huh?" Curtis asked shakily.

Now Murphy smiled slightly.

"You didn't really think I'd let you go alone, did you?"

The facade Curtis' face displayed began to crumble. He glanced about wildly, trying to figure out who had spied on him.

Murphy chuckled and looked around at his men as well.

"Dallas, come here my boy."

Dallas Hildebrand strolled over cockily out of the shadows and stood beside his boss. Murphy propped his arm on Hildebrand's shoulder and looked at him.

"What'd you see in town the other night?"

Dallas relished the opportunity to be of service to Murphy and it showed in his voice as he presented his observations. He sounded almost giddy.

"Saw Talmadge Barkhouse sneaking in the back door of the church right before dark."

"And..." Murphy led him along.

"Wouldn't have thought much of it. Talmadge and the preacher are friends, right?

"Oh, sure," Murphy said teasingly.

He and Hildebrand flashed nasty grins at Curtis now.

"Problem is," Dallas continued. "A certain black fella we all well know very well soon joined him."

"He's a liar!" Curtis screamed.

Curtis knew that it wasn't a lie, but he had to try something. He had to hopefully create a little doubt in Murphy's mind.

"Am I?" Dallas asked Curtis confidently.

Curtis couldn't meet his gaze, much less answer him. He just hung his head.

"I reckon that's settled," Dallas told Murphy, still grinning.

Murphy nodded and glared at Curtis.

"You wanna tell me what y'all were talking about that was so secretive you had to go sneaking around in the dark?" he asked.

Curtis shook his head.

"It would behoove you to answer me Curtis. Quick and honest."

Curtis knew that he was in a jackpot now. He wished with everything in him that he'd have just come down shooting. Now, there was nothing he could do to save himself. All he could do was stay quiet. Telling Murphy something he already knew would do him no favors, and possibly make things worse.

"I don't know what Dallas is talking 'bout," he mumbled. "I never saw Talmadge at the church."

He hated to lie. He believed the Bible, every word of it and it said not to lie. Silently, he prayed that God would forgive him just this once. Lying had never been a habit of his.

Meanwhile, Murphy became more impatient. He'd give Curtis one more chance to give him what he wanted before he'd take it.

"You sure about that?" he asked Curtis.

Curtis nodded, but never picked up his head. Murphy motioned Dallas to do something and Dallas didn't hesitate to comply.

He stood dead in front of Curtis until he finally looked up. When he did, Dallas buried a breathtaking uppercut in Curtis' gut. He coughed hard and fell to a knee. As he got to his feet, Dallas repeated the blow. This one put Curtis on all fours.

"Thomas," Murphy called. "Grab that rope behind you."

Thomas Taylor did as he was instructed and retrieved the rope Murphy had referred to from the back wall.

"Tie me a noose in it," Murphy instructed.

Thomas set about fashioning the noose that Murphy wanted. Curtis looked up at Murphy following this command and Dallas kicked him in the mouth for his troubles.

Next, Murphy called over Jeremiah Cook. Besides being hired because he was Gene's brother, he'd been kept around for his physicality. He was a hulking beast of a man with grizzly paws for hands. Jeremiah stood a couple inches taller than Murphy even, looked as if he was a couple of ax-handles broad at the shoulders, and if his body held any fat, you couldn't see it.

He walked over and stood beside his boss, awaiting instruction.

"Get him talking," was all Murphy had to say.

Jeremiah stomped over and grabbed Curtis by the back of his collar and stood him on his feet single-handedly. Curtis didn't stay there long though as thundering punch hit him square in the forehead, making everything spin.

Once again, Jeremiah lifted him, this time hammering in the chest. Curtis heaved. He couldn't have spoken at that point if he wanted to. He writhed on the ground and managed to roll over to his back. He felt like a turtle on its shell, not sure if he'd ever be upright again. The light from the lanterns were enough to make his pounding head hurt worse.

The others looked on, some grimacing as Jeremiah squatted over his prey. Watching the beast of a man tear apart another human sounded fun in theory, but it was a gruesome thing in practice. He grabbed Curtis again, this time by the front of his collar, and pulled him to him a bit.

"Boss wants you to talk," Jeremiah told him menacingly. "Or I'm gonna start hurtin' ya."

Curtis hated to think of what might be in his future if the pain had yet to begin. Thomas Taylor's voice broke the quiet before he could find out.

"Rope's ready!"

"Bring it on over," Murphy said.

Thomas did just that and handed the rope over to Murphy. Jeremiah stood from over Curtis and stepped aside. Curtis couldn't speak, only scream internally as he sucked in slight gulps of air.

Murphy tossed the untied end of his rope over the rafter above his head and looped the noose around Curtis' neck. Curtis tried to fight it, but he had no chance.

"Get him up!" Murphy said to just anybody as he stepped back.

Phillip Clark and Preston pulled tightly on the rope until they had Curtis on his feet. His fingers fought desperately at the rope around his throat as it bit in.

Murphy motioned with his hands to lower him just a little. They did and Murphy nodded in approval.

"Jeremiah…" Murphy said, gesturing toward Curtis.

Jeremiah knew just what to do and restarted his work.

His monstrous fists began to pound Curtis all over his face and body. He ripped open Curtis' shirt so he could see the skin ripple and tear as he hit him. The blows began to leave their mark as blood, bruising, and swelling began to appear.

Curtis' nose was a broken mess and both of his eyes were nearly swollen shut. He had cuts on both cheekbones and his mouth oozed blood. Within a matter of minutes, he was unrecognizable.

Murphy knew that he had to stop this monster before he killed Curtis. He wanted to hear him say that it was him that betrayed him and if the beating didn't stop soon, he never have that chance.

"That's enough!" he yelled.

Jeremiah threw one last punch as he pulled himself away from Curtis. His chest was heaving and he was drenched in blood and sweat. Only his brother Gene had ever seen him beat a man like this and it nearly turned a few of their stomachs.

"Drop him," Murphy said.

Phillip and Preston gladly released the end of the rope and let Curtis fall. When he did fall, he went right to his knees, his torso rocking back and forth slightly. Murphy grabbed a stool and took a seat on it right in front of Curtis.

"You know," he said. "It didn't have to be this way Curtis. Hell, I ain't even mad that you told him. He knew anyway. I just want to hear you say it."

Curtis' mind spun wildly as he tried to make sense of the words he heard. He was barely conscious, barely alive. Murphy even thought he was dead for a moment, grabbing his arm to keep him from tipping over. He couldn't open his eyes if he tried. They were as big as oranges and completely swollen shut. His mouth was busted wide open and it was all he could do to keep from swallowing his own blood.

But suddenly, for some reason, it was as if his mind could no longer force his mouth to not tell Murphy everything. He tried to stop himself from saying it as he heard the words aloud, but it was too late.

His words weren't loud or clear, and Murphy had to lean in close to hear them, but the truth was told.

"I... I... I told him," Curtis said.

He took a shallow breath and spoke again, his words barely audible.

"I was... testify. He's... Miles City... lawyer."

Murphy sat back, almost amazed.

"Did you say Talmadge is gone to Miles City to get a lawyer and you were gonna testify?"

He leaned back in to hear Curtis' response.

"Uh huh," was all he could muster.

Murphy had heard all that he needed, which was a good thing because Curtis was done. His brain was rattled beyond repair. He was losing control of his body fast. Death wasn't far.

Murphy stood to his feet and put his stool back where'd gotten it from. He stared down at Curtis, deciding whether or not to put him out of his misery.

"One more," he told Jeremiah.

Jeremiah was more than happy to oblige. He let out an inhuman grunt as he reared back his fist and planted the finishing blow to the side of Curtis' head. There was a thud and a loud crack as Curtis' body fell limp on its side. Just like that, Curtis was dead.

Everyone stood in stunned silence. It was probably the most barbaric death that any of them had ever witnessed and possibly brought about a new fearful respect for Jeremiah.

The only thing that Murphy was concerned with was that he had gotten what he wanted and that he now knew that Talmadge was not at home. His plans for the night had been quickly changed.

It was the early hours of the next morning with no daylight coming soon and all was quiet at the Barkhouse residence. Everyone but Orel was sound asleep. He hadn't slept a wink as his nerves just wouldn't allow it. Things had been surprisingly quiet in the days since Augustus had killed Adam Lewis, and he just didn't trust it.

Orel's suspicions of the unexpected quietness were proven true as the thunder of horses' hooves came within earshot. It didn't take long for him to distinguish just what the sound was and that trouble was coming with it.

"Lake!" he called out loudly as he sprung from his bed.

His eldest brother was asleep on a cot beside their parents' bed in the main bedroom in their father's absence.

Orel burst through the door, yelling that Murphy's men were coming.

A stunned and sleepy Lake rose up in confusion. The night had gone from completely silent to being interrupted by Orel's screams. Belle sat up in bed and rubbed her eyes.

"What's going on?" she mumbled sleepily.

Just then, the first shot rang out and a bullet pelted the side of the house.

"It's Murphy's men!" Orel yelled back.

By now, Lake had somewhat gathered himself and grabbed a shotgun from beside the bed. He handed it to his mother and barked his commands.

"Take that and get on the floor!"

His words were harsh, but she understood the gravity of the situation that led to their harshness. Lake was in charge with Talmadge away and she did as she was told, just like she would for her husband.

More shots sounded off as Chauncey and Avery emerged from their bedroom, armed. A bullet shattered a window and Lake swung the front door open. He shot wildly at half-lit figures that rambled about on horseback in front of him. The only things he could see for sure were the flashes coming from the muzzles of their guns.

The other brothers shot back from various windows around the house. Shattering glass flying at his face sent Chauncey reeling.

"You okay?" Lake hollered back to him.

"Yea!"

The sound of gunfire began to grow further away back behind the house. Orel had grown tired of being ambushed. He was just mad enough to want to strike back and he planned to do it now. He expelled the used up casings from his revolver and shuffled for more to take their place. When he had his gun reloaded, he stormed toward the front door. His mother called after him, but he never heard her.

Lake had just closed the door when Orel slammed it back open.

"What are you doing?" he asked Orel.

It was as if Lake wasn't even on the same planet as Orel when he brushed by him. Barefooted as a yard dog and in his night clothes, Orel sprinted for the stables.

"Orel, no!" Lake screamed to no avail.

"Where's he going, Lake?" Belle asked.

"I don't know, Mama."

"Well go after him, please!" she pleaded.

Lake did as she requested, but he was way behind.

Orel had grabbed the first horse he could and mounted it without a saddle or any other gear. With his left hand wrapped tightly in the mane of the horse and his pistol tightly gripped in his right, Orel rode north in the same direction where the sounds of shooting had faded. Not far behind the house, his horse half stumbled, half leapt over something that he couldn't quite make out. He quickly righted the horse on its path and headed after the assailants.

After a few hundred yards, he began to see the glow of lantern light ahead and kicked the horse on faster. He was gaining ground at a hurried pace when voices began to be loud enough to hear.

"Someone's coming!" he heard one of them warn.

The rest of the voices were one great, muddled mess. He had gotten close enough that he slowed the horse back to a gallop so he could shoot at least semi-accurately. His pistol was aimed, rising and falling with each lope. He picked a silhouette, aimed as best he could and fired. His aim was off as they had begun to move faster.

He lined his shot up again, and this time it was true. A pained groan was let out in the dark and Orel tried to find another target. His horse fought him though, bucking at the gunfire.

Murphy's men, realizing they had a significant numbers advantage and that Orel was struggling with his horse, stopped and turned to return fire.

Orel gained control back of the horse just in time to go headlong into a volley of gunfire. Bullets and buckshot whizzed by and the horse whined as if possibly hit. He looked down at the horse when he suddenly felt the thud of a rifle bullet smack his left shoulder. His grip on the horse's mane was gone and he felt his body beginning to slip backwards. The pistol in Orel's hand blasted as he attempted to drop it. The tips of his right fingers had barely brushed the horse's mane when it bucked again. Now, there was nothing he could do. He landed back first in the weeds, and dirt, and briers.

On the ground, he searched for his gun as the last of the bullets pelted the ground around him. He felt the warm steel with his fingers and sat up straight just in time to catch a glancing blow from a horse's hoof to his temple. Blood leaked from his head and shoulder; he was out like a light.

Murphy's men took this as an opportunity to head for home. They'd done what they came to do and possibly more. Their boss would be well-pleased with the job they'd done.

As they rode off into the night, Lake finally made it to his brother's side.

Orel was out cold and barely breathing. The upper part of his night clothes were already drenched in blood from his shoulder and he laid in a pool of it from his head wound. There was a noticeable indention where the horse's hoof had caught him. Lake tried to compose himself as tears began to fill his eyes. He hated to think it, but he knew that there was no way his baby brother's prognosis could be anything but fatal.

"Come on, Orel. Please," he said hopelessly.

As he tried to scoop his body up, the other brothers arrived on horseback. They quickly swung down to see how they could possibly help. Both Chauncey and Avery knew immediately that it wasn't good.

"Oh, God," said Chauncey as if he might be sick.

"I'm gonna get on one of these horses. Y'all lift him up to me," Lake instructed.

In a flash, the eldest of the Barkhouse brothers was on a horse and awaiting the body of the youngest.

Painstakingly, Chauncey and Avery lifted Orel's body up onto the horse with Lake. His entire body was limp, but his shoulder was another matter entirely. The bullet had found its mark and done its job. Lake could feel the bones moving about unnaturally and his head looked about as badly as a kick to the head from a horse could be expected to look.

Lake headed for home, praying and whispering reassuring words to his brother all the way as he cradled him to his chest like a mother may hold a newborn. Chauncey and Avery rode back double as there was no sign of Orel's spooked horse.

One look at Orel was enough to send Belle to the floor in hysteria as Lake carried him through the front door. She thought him dead.

"He ain't dead, Mama," Lake sniffled. "Not yet."

Although she knew the same exact thing about Orel's outlook that Lake did, the fact that he was yet to be gone gave her the strength to pull herself together.

"Lay him on my bed," she told him, wiping tears from her face.

Lake did so gladly. In all the fuss, he'd twisted his back and the weight of his stocky younger brother was taking its toll.

Belle fetched some water and a cloth, wiping Orel's head as clean as possible. Through the rag, she could feel the deformity that the horse's hoof had caused to his head. This, once again, brought tears to her eyes.

"Help me get these clothes off of him," she said.

"I wouldn't bother with that shoulder, Mama," Lake replied.

Belle shot him a look that immediately told him that his mind had been changed for him. He quickly understood that his mother's words were not a request.

"If he's gonna die on us here, he's gonna die washed and in clean clothes." She said matter-of-factly.

Avery and Chauncey arrived and helped their mother, seeing the shape that Lake's back was in. They stripped him and Belle bathed him. She cleaned, packed, and dressed the shoulder wound as best she could, and wrapped his head.

When he'd been washed to her standards, Belle helped them dress him in his finest clothes. These would be his burial clothes and they all knew it. His body had slowed down so much that his blood was barely pumping, so the blood seeping through into his shirt wasn't much of a worry. The slug was bulging at the edge of the skin in the mangled shoulder blade, preventing blood from escaping that way.

Once she had Orel settled, Belle climbed up in bed beside her soon to be dead son and laid down. She held onto his hand, stroking his hair and softly singing hymns. He was all she had left of her dearly departed father, who Orel resembled so much, both in looks and mannerisms.

The two of them laid that way until she drifted off to sleep, unable to resist the mental and physical exhaustion any longer.

Shortly after daybreak, Lake sent Chauncey and Avery out to check on the herd. He didn't know what else to do at this point so he sat in a chair by his brother's side, occasionally nodding off to sleep.

A sudden deeper breath, deeper than he'd breathed since he'd been hurt, came from Orel, startling his brother awake. This would be his last.

Lake checked for signs of life, but found none. The inevitable had happened: Orel Barkhouse was dead.

Belle was still asleep so Lake chose not to wake her up at the moment. Instead, he allowed her to rest as peacefully as she could, holding on to her baby boy.

***

Without a clue of what happened during their absence, Talmadge and Augustus Barkhouse rode happily along toward home a couple of days later. Talmadge even whistled a bit, a usual practice of his before all the chaos had broken loose. He was able to push the loss of one son to the back of his mind briefly, filled with the thought that justice may soon be served.

He no longer feared for Gus' life and they'd both be going back where they belonged. His peace, however, began to unravel a little over a mile from home.

The smell of some sort of rotting flesh filled the air, overtaking their nostrils.

"You smell that, Pa?" Gus asked.

"Sure do," he replied. "Something's dead for sure."

They circled around, trying to identify the direction that the smell appeared to be coming from. Talmadge happened to think about a wallow that may be holding water to their east. He knew that a dying animal was likely to head for water if it knew its fate.

"Follow me," he told Gus as he rode east.

Sure enough, the scent grew stronger the further they headed in that direction. A gentle breeze out of the east held the stench in the air. Once he could see the wallow, Talmadge also saw the source of the smell that led them there.

The horse Orel had ridden after Murphy Cole's men laid dead beside the muddy hole that was all but empty of water.

"That looks like one of our horses!" Augustus shouted.

"Sure does," Talmadge concurred.

He was perplexed as to why one of their horses would be away from home and lying dead near water as if it had been injured. He thought for sure that one of the boys would know that the horse was gone. His excitement over the prospect of being able to actually take down Cole had caused him to temporarily forget about everything that could have happened while they'd been gone.

All of those possibilities came flooding back as they approached the rotting horse. The increasingly warmer temperatures of late spring caused the flesh to decay faster.

Talmadge's heart sank like an anchor at sea upon discovering the bullet hole in the mare's brisket. He swung down off his horse to take a closer look, covering his nose and mouth with his kerchief in an attempt to keep the smell out.

"She's been shot," he said solemnly as he knelt beside her.

Augustus didn't say anything, he only dropped his head and shook it.

"Had to be Murphy's men," Talmadge added.

"No doubt about that," Gus said.

Talmadge patted the horse a time or two and rose quickly to get back on his horse.

"I don't like this one bit," he said. "We've got to get home to make sure everything's alright there."

Gus nodded in agreement and they rode off toward home at a brisk pace.

They'd crested the rolling hill behind their home when the scent of something rotting once again filled their nostrils. More dead animals was the first thing that popped into Talmadge's head. He wished he'd been right about that when he realized that the actual source of the smell was a dead body.

"Christ, almighty!" he exclaimed. "It's Curtis!"

Augustus could hardly believe that his father had used the name of God in such a way, but he undoubtedly understood why he had.

Lying amongst the grass and briers was the swollen body of Black Curtis. He'd been beaten to a pulp by Jeremiah, but identifying the only black man around wasn't difficult. Both of them knew that this was not a good sign of things to be found inside the home. They shared a knowing glance and set off for the house with the horses at full speed.

Talmadge slid his horse in sideways in front of the house, kicking up dust as he dismounted. As he approached the door, Lake flung it open with a rifle in hand. There was a fleeting look of relief in his eyes at the sight of his father, but the moment didn't last long at all. Talmadge could tell that something was wrong with the family just by looking at his oldest boy.

"What's wrong?" he asked as he brushed by Lake into the house.

Inside, he saw exactly what was wrong. Orel was laid out on the bed with his mother sitting by his side. They'd done their best to keep his body cool, but the house had begun to carry the smell of death.

Belle looked up at Talmadge and when their eyes met, they both burst into tears. She stood to her feet, but fell right into her husband's arms. They stood beside the body of their dead son, holding each other and sobbing.

Augustus came into the house and upon seeing Orel dead, immediately felt a lump in his throat. Warm water ran in his mouth and he felt weak in the knees. He bolted haphazardly back outside where he began to vomit. It felt as if everything he'd ever eaten was trying to come out all at once. When he was empty, he heaved and heaved until his breath left him. Lake grabbed him gently by the shoulders and tried to stand him upright so he could hopefully take in some air.

Gus' body hurt him all over as he tried to regain his composure. He broke out in a cold sweat and felt as if his heart would beat out of his chest. He welcomed it though. His mind was having an easier time pondering what ifs than it was trying to rectify its own issues right now.

He thought that maybe Murphy Cole had gotten what he wanted by killing Asa and Simon. Maybe he'd sent the message he had planned for them and it was going to be over. But no, he'd had to kill Adam Lewis like a fool. He'd brought this hell on them. Another brother and a fine man were dead because of him.

If he'd had any idea of what plans Murphy Cole truly had or had he been able to truly think clearly, he'd know that this wasn't the case at all. He was just in a state of panic right now.

But suddenly, he wasn't. With his mind preoccupied, his body had seemingly righted itself. His heartbeat was normal again and he was no longer heaving. He just sat on the ground, numb.

"You alright?" Lake asked him.

Augustus just nodded.

"Where's Chauncey and Avery?"

"They're gone over to Claire's."

Augustus nodded again.

Talmadge came out of the house. He'd settled himself and Belle down enough now to come and get the story of what happened from Lake.

"Where are the other boys?" he asked as he approached.

"Gone to Claire's to tell her and Luke about Orel," Lake replied.

Talmadge looked back at the house and noticed the fresh bullet holes for the first time.

"They came night before last," Lake said. "Orel went after 'em on a horse. I tried to get to him, but he went quick and didn't even saddle up."

Talmadge and Gus shared a look.

"I reckon that explains the dead horse," Gus said.

Lake seemed surprised.

"So they killed the horse too?" he asked.

"Yea," Talmadge told him. "Found her dead by the old elk wallow, bullet hole in her brisket."

This made sense to Lake. He'd heard the horse make a distressed noise as he'd closed in on where Orel was.

"I was too worried about Orel to care about the horse," he told them as he leaned on the rifle for support.

"What happened to your back?" Gus asked him.

"Twisted it in all the mess the other night. Ain't been worth a lick since."

Talmadge stood there mulling things over, especially trying to sort out how Curtis had gotten tied up in the whole affair. If Cole had found out their plan, him killing Curtis made sense, but why hadn't Lake mentioned it?

"So, was Curtis here with y'all?" Talmadge asked.

Now it was Lake's turn to be perplexed. Why would Curtis be here? He knew the plan, but didn't understand what Curtis had to do with Orel being dead. Had Curtis betrayed them? Surely not. It just wasn't in his makeup.

"Curtis?" Lake stammered. "No. Why?"

Now everyone was confused.

"Well he's lying dead a couple hundred yards behind the house," Talmadge informed him.

Lake was bewildered. He'd had no idea that Curtis was even around, much less dead within a few hundred yards of the house. His mind went in a million different directions trying to parse this out. His father and brother were just as confused as he was.

Finally, Lake's brain came across a possible answer to their question.

"He have a rope around his neck?" he asked.

Both Talmadge and Augustus had to think on it as they had been in such a hurry to get home to check on their family.

"Matter of fact, I think he did. Why?" asked Gus.

"I'll bet they done him the same way they done Asa and Simon," Lake responded.

This made a lot of sense other than one detail.

"He weren't shot though, was he?" Gus asked Talmadge.

"No," he said. "But somebody had sure beat him. I mean it looked like they'd done it with their fists, but who could do that?"

Lake's mind went immediately to Jeremiah Cook.

"What's that younger Cook fella that works for Cole's name?" he asked them.

"Jeremiah?" Gus thought aloud.

"Yea, him. He could have done it."

Talmadge nodded in agreement.

"Yea," he agreed. "He's a load."

Their inferences were all correct, but they did nothing to improve their situation. In fact, everything had gone downhill since Talmadge had received the good news from the lawyer in Miles City. That was all down the drain now. There wouldn't be any court case. Murphy Cole would not have his just deserts meted out by the law. Any potential justice would have to be served frontier style. Talmadge knew that bloodshed was the only possible way that this could play out without tucking tail and running. That was not an option he had though.

# Chapter Fourteen

Montgomery Cole's heart and mind were heavily burdened as he rode toward his brother's ranch atop his typically borrowed horse. His allegiances to his family, his friends, and to God, were all pulling him in three different directions.

"Come on in, Uncle Monty," Preston said as he opened the front door to welcome their visitor.

It was late evening when he arrived, which meant there was only one place that his brother would be.

"Pa's in the den having a whiskey and a cigar," Preston informed him.

"Oh, I'm sure he is," Monty laughed.

Preston went ahead of him, leading the way although his uncle knew full well where to go.

"Uncle Monty's here," Preston informed his father.

"So I heard," Murphy replied dryly.

Monty walked into his brother's den knowing all too well that he was not welcomed there. Murphy had never particularly cared for his older brother and his becoming a preacher hadn't helped their relationship. Really, the only 'friend' that Murphy had was possibly Gene Cook. Gene had worked for him for many years and they shared a bond not common between Murphy and his other employees. His other brothers were family and pawns used by him to play the game of chess he was constantly working in his mind. Montgomery was on the outside looking in on the Cole family due to his resistance to following Murphy's lead.

"What brings you here, Preacher?" Murphy asked between pulls on his cigar.

It was just a small thing, but they both knew him calling Monty 'Preacher' was just a verbal jab referencing their lack of closeness as family.

"I've come to talk to you about all that's been going on," Monty replied, acting as if his brother's addressing of him hadn't bothered him.

"And what might that be?" Murphy asked facetiously, a big smile on his face.

Monty slipped his coat off and took a seat across from his brother. He could tell right away that Murphy didn't care to be in his presence for any extended period of time. Truth be told, he had no desire to be there either, and wouldn't be if he didn't feel so led.

"Look," he started. "You can cut the games with me. We both know that I know what's going on."

Murphy Cole didn't take kindly to being spoken to that way, much less in his own home. He bit down hard on his cigar before downing the rest of his whiskey in a single swallow.

"No, you look. I don't know what you're talking about. I thought that was clear."

It would have been quite easy for the preacher to lose his composure. Lying and being made out to be a fool were two things he wouldn't abide by, and neither would any other self-respecting man.

"I'm no fool, Murphy. I'm a man just like you are. Just because I don't kill people doesn't make me any less of one.

Murphy tried to feign offense.

"I haven't killed a soul."

"But you've had it done," Monty fired back.

"Says who?"

Murphy knew his routine of playing dumb was an easy way to get under Monty's skin. He was a man of the Lord, but one undeniable trait of a Cole that Montgomery did have was a fiery temper. His ability to control his was just a bit better than the others.

"You tell me how Orel Barkhouse ended up dead, then. Curtis, too," he challenged.

"Well I'd heard about the Barkhouse boy, but I didn't know Curtis was dead. He lit out from here a little while back."

They both knew it was a lie, but Monty wondered if he had to make it so obvious.

"So you're telling me you don't know anything about either one of them getting killed?" Monty pushed on.

"That's right," he lied. "And I don't appreciate what you're insinuating."

"And what's that?"

He knew Murphy was getting low on patience, but he also knew that this could work in his favor as Murphy was wont to become more loose-lipped with anger.

"You know damn well, preacher man."

"There's no call for that kind of talk," Monty fired back.

"No," Murphy replied as he stood to his feet. "There's no call to come in a man's house and accuse him of the sort of things you're accusing me of."

Murphy stepped closer to Monty in an attempt to intimidate him. He was a big man and was never shy about throwing his weight around. He knew his older brother wouldn't threaten him physically. It wasn't for fear of him as Murphy wished to believe, but simply his nature and standing as a pastor.

Monty also stood and glared back at his brother.

"I'll never understand why you do the things that you do," he said as he reached for his coat.

Monty walked toward the door to see himself out as Murphy spoke, causing him to stop and look back.

"Everything I do, I do for this family. But you wouldn't know about that, would you? You left us to go follow God. Well to Hell with you and God!"

Murphy stomped off to his bedroom while Monty stomped out the front door. A brotherhood that had never been very strong may have just been destroyed beyond repair.

# Chapter Fifteen

Talmadge was at a loss. He didn't know how to make himself, his children, or his wife feel better. All that they could do was hurt. It had been bad enough when Asa and Simon were killed, but it seemed as if every move they had made since had been a misstep.

At this point, he was ready to make a drastic move. He knew Belle wouldn't be happy, but she wasn't now, so why not at least try?

"Where you going?"

His wife's voice caught Talmadge off guard. He spun around on his heels to face her. The look on his face told her that he didn't want to answer her question. Instead, he turned his attention back to securing the horse to the buckboard he'd been loading. Belle did not take kindly to being ignored.

"I'm talking to you, Tal," she said loudly.

Once again, he turned to face her, still not wanting to answer. Belle just stared at him, trying to get a read on what he had on his mind. When he couldn't hold her look, her heart sank. She knew that something was amiss, but now she was genuinely afraid of just what he had planned.

As he turned away again, she stepped forward to have a look at what he had loaded into the wagon. Peeling back a blanket, she uncovered a small arsenal of weapons including two rifles, a shotgun, and four pistols.

"No!" she screamed.

Talmadge never even acknowledged her outburst as he walked into the house to grab the last of what needed.

Belle turned quickly as she saw Lake and Avery coming around from the barn leading their horses with Chauncey following behind. Tears began to stream from her eyes as the reality of what she knew was about to happen set in. They were tears of both anger and despair.

When Talmadge emerged from the house, Belle met him in a full run, slapping him in his chest in a fit of rage and heartache.

"Woman, have you lost your mind?" he asked, pushing her back and holding her at arm's length.

"I won't let you do it!" she managed through her sobs.

Talmadge let her go and the pair just stared at each other.

"Nothing's gonna happen," he lied, hoping to calm her.

It was to no avail. Belle knew what all of this meant and no thinly veiled attempt to comfort her would work.

"You know exactly what you're doing!" she yelled at him.

"And what's that, Belle?" Talmadge fired back.

For a few moments, she didn't say a word, only stared at him incredulously. They both knew that there was nothing but trouble to come from the plans that Talmadge had.

"You're gonna get our boys killed!" Belle cried. "And yourself too."

"We're not going looking for trouble, sweetheart. We've got business in town."

"And what business is that, Tal?" she snapped.

He looked at her again, this time directly in her eyes. He knew she was worried, but now he could see just how deep that concern ran. There had to be something he could do to lessen this worry, but he didn't know what. Truth be told, he was worried too. His hope was that their trip to Langston would be uneventful, but the chances of that were very slim to none.

"Look," Talmadge told her as he pulled his shirt away from his chest, revealing that it could be seen through.

Belle looked ashamed. The very clothes that she'd stitched herself were almost reduced to being just thread. She was failing in her responsibility to clothe her family and it broke her heart.

"We've got to get those supplies. We need 'em. Our boys need 'em."

She nodded as a few tears escaped her eyes. Talmadge reached up and gently brushed them away and pulled her into his chest.

"Are you just gonna leave me here alone?" Belle asked in one last attempt to make him stay.

"Of course not," he replied as they separated from each other's embrace. "Gus will be here. I figure it's best he don't show in town for a while. Plus, Claire and Luke are coming to see you!"

Her eyes lit up. Although they didn't live far, a newlywed couple of less than a year needed their own time and space. Any visit from them was a welcomed one.

"Matter of fact, here they come now."

Talmadge pointed back beyond the house where Luke and Claire approached in their wagon.

When they'd all said their hellos and goodbyes, Talmadge and the boys headed off for town, leaving Luke and Augustus to look after the ladies.

Langston was fairly quiet when the Barkhouse men arrived, a fact much appreciated by Talmadge. Prior to entering the town, they'd stopped long enough to arm themselves with their handguns. Though the trip was innocent enough, it was very apt to turn violent and they had no intentions of being unprepared. Regardless, the presence of one certain individual all but guaranteed that blood would be shed that day.

Unseen by the Barkhouses, Phillip Clark lingered outside Melvin Cole's saloon down the street. Having been knocked unconscious by Augustus the day that Adam Lewis was killed, he had a specific ax to grind with the entire Barkhouse family. Vengeance was on his mind and he'd had just enough liquor to make him bold enough to act on it without any orders from his boss.

Inside, the purchase went off without a hitch. Sharon had instructed Tom to set the items aside that Talmadge and Belle had intended to purchase previously.

"I certainly appreciate it," Talmadge told them.

"I told Tom you'd be back to get those things," Sharon said. "They've been waiting for you all along."

"And I appreciate you selling to us," Talmadge continued. "I'm sure we're not easy friends to have right now."

"Don't you ever worry about that Tal. Long as we're here, you've got friends in Langston," Tom assured him.

This was very comforting to their ears. They stood around and made small talk for a few minutes before Talmadge figured they'd been in public long enough.

"Well I do hate to be rude, but we probably ought to be going, things like they are."

He motioned to the materials which Chauncey and Avery grabbed, then led the way out the door with his sons in tow. What they found on the other side of that door was quite unexpected and unfriendly.

Their time in the Waltons' store hadn't been long, but it was time enough for Phillip Clark to assemble two of his comrades. Clark himself stood not ten feet away down the sidewalk. Thomas Taylor sat aboard their buggy as if awaiting a ride and Frank Hall leaned against the edge of the building just to their right and slightly closer.

Talmadge screeched to a halt upon seeing them, first Taylor then the others.

"Gentlemen," he said calmly as he steadied himself.

No one else made a peep. Talmadge had thought that maybe with the store being so near to the edge of town, they'd slip in and out unseen. He'd also wanted them to stay together and didn't leave anyone outside to watch; a decision he now realized was a mistake.

Clark's eyes were locked on Chauncey as he had been with his brother when he killed Adam Lewis. His revenge would be carried out on the closest alternative possible, outnumbered or not. Chauncey must have felt his stare as his previously darting eyes now trained themselves right back on Clark. Still, nobody said a word.

"We're just here to buy these supplies. We ain't looking for no trouble," Talmadge tried again.

"I don't give a damn what you are or ain't looking for," Clark growled. "You started trouble last you were here and I aim to finish it now."

Talmadge wanted to tell him what he already knew but wouldn't admit; how his boss was the one that had started all of this and how they were only fighting back. There was plenty Talmadge wanted to say, but he was trying his best to diffuse the situation. He knew that even though they had the numbers, there was no way they'd come out of this unscathed.

"If you'll just let us take our things and go, nobody don't have to get hurt," he continued.

Clark just laughed. His mind was made up from the moment he'd seen them from down the street. Hall and Thomas were willing participants as well.

"Ain't nobody I care about gonna get hurt," Clark sneered arrogantly.

"Now you know good as I do, there ain't no way you or your men don't get hurt too," Talmadge replied. "So if you'll just let us..."

"You heard him," Hall interrupted.

That sealed it for Talmadge. It was now beyond Clark mouthing off. His backup stood by until now, but his voice had been raised in agreement. The time for idle talk was over. Everyone knew it, including those simply watching. Once the silence fell again, the street cleared.

Now it was just a matter of who would pull first and when he'd do it. Everyone's minds raced as they tried to figure out a course of action. Eyes darted all about except Chauncey and Phillip Clark who glared at each other. It began to feel as if nothing would ever happen.

And then, in a flash, it did.

Clark drew and his aim was true, likely a fatal blow to Chauncey's sternum had he not been carrying the bundle of material in his arm which stopped the bullet.

Lake was a step or two behind the others and had a clear bead on Frank Hall, who he shot squarely in the shoulder, dropping him to a knee.

Talmadge and Thomas Taylor exchanged wild gunfire, missing each other with several shots.

By the time Chauncey could drop the materials, draw, roll to his right, and return fire, one of Avery's bullets found its mark in Clark's gut. He stumbled back and shot quickly back in Avery's direction. It was a lucky shot, striking him almost dead center in the forehead and killing him instantly.

All three of the other Barkhouses were momentarily stunned at realizing that Avery had been killed. Clark took advantage, whizzing a bullet by Talmadge's ear close enough to nick it. With fire in his eyes, Talmadge turned back and placed two rounds in Clark's chest, finishing him. His hammer fell on an empty chamber next.

Taylor shot at him from the other side of the buckboard, but had his fire returned by Chauncey.

Lake took this opportunity to slip up to the back of the wagon and grab the shotgun. Cocking the hammers back, he rolled around the edge of the wagon where Taylor was reloading. Lake let him hold both barrels at almost point blank range and nearly decapitated him.

Things had calmed down by now. The gunfire had ceased, but its echo and aroma still hung heavy in the air. The horses that were on their own had managed to run off, but the one tied to the buckboard had barely flinched despite the racket.

Frank Hall had all but been forgotten until Lake came around the front of the buckboard and was met by a bullet in his chest that exploded his heart.

Hall had managed to get himself back to his feet, but he wouldn't be there for long. Talmadge and Chauncey turned and slammed him with a volley of shots that very well may have taken down an elephant.

As smoke from the heated battle slowly dissipated, the two men left standing quietly took inventory of the carnage surrounding them. Five men lay dead in an area less than thirty yards square. In terms of the number of casualties, they had won three to two, but this was no victory.

It had only taken two bullets finding their mark to kill Avery and Lake but they were just as dead as their bullet-riddled adversaries. All told, Phillip Clark had been struck three times while seven slugs had found their mark in the body of Frank Hall. Thomas Taylor was sprawled out unrecognizable in the street by the Barkhouses' buckboard, his head laid open from the shotgun blast. Close quarters battle was fast and brutal.

"We need to go," Talmadge said, breaking the eerie silence.

Chauncey just stood there, stunned. His eyes darted back and forth between the bodies of his brothers but he was a million miles away mentally.

"Chauncey," Talmadge tried again.

This time he got his attention.

"Yea?" Chauncey asked.

"We have got to go."

He just nodded as they began to quickly load Avery and Lake's bodies into the wagon. A crowd had begun to fill the streets as they sped away out of town, once again leaving the materials they had bought behind. Their scattered horses weren't even an afterthought.

***

It didn't take long for news of what had occurred to reach Murphy Cole. Preston was coming in from checking on the cattle when he surprisingly met his uncle Milo approaching the house at a hurried pace. Right away, he knew that something was wrong.

"What's going on?" he asked as he led his horse out to meet his uncle.

Milo just dropped his head and continued on toward the house.

"Uncle Milo," Preston urged to no avail.

He turned his horse back behind Milo and followed him on back.

"I need to see your pa," Milo said as he dismounted.

"He's inside," Preston informed him. "What's going on?"

Still Milo didn't answer. He just handed the reigns of his horse to Preston and let himself in the house. Preston dropped both sets of reins and went right on in behind him.

"Murphy!" Milo called out.

He didn't even realize that his brother was sitting right there in the same room.

"What in the hell do you want, Milo?" he asked without looking up.

Milo's voice failed him as he stood in silence, much to the annoyance of Murphy. When Milo still didn't speak for several moments, Murphy finally looked up. As soon as he locked eyes on his brother, he knew that bad news had brought him there.

"What's wrong?" he asked as he rose from his chair.

"There's... there's," Milo stammered.

Murphy backhanded his brother sharply, attempting to set his mind straight. Preston flinched at the blow and Milo took a step back.

"There's what, dammit?" Murphy demanded.

Now Milo found his nerve.

"There's been a shooting in town. The Barkhouses and some of your men."

"Who's dead?"

"Two of the Barkhouses and three of yours."

"Phillip's gotta be one of 'em," Preston interjected. "I know he'd gone to town."

"Uh huh," Milo said. "Taylor and Hall too."

Murphy stood in silence, mulling over this new information. He couldn't believe those cowpunchers had fared so well against his men. They were cattlemen too, but first and foremost, they were deadly. How they'd managed to be outgunned was beyond him. Something just wasn't right. He was a bit sad at first, but now he was mad.

He snarled at Milo who stood waiting for some response. What he got was a stiff right hand that put him on the seat of his britches.

"And where were you?" he yelled at Milo.

Milo tried to stand, but Murphy knocked him down once more.

"Pa!" Preston yelled.

"Shut up, boy!" he fired back.

The look his father gave him told Preston that he was in no mood to be messed with. Murphy Cole was a frightening man when he was in this state of mind.

Again, Milo tried to stand, only to have his legs kicked out from under him.

"I asked you a question. I didn't tell you to stand up."

Milo looked up at Murphy through his already swelling eye.

"I didn't know what was going on."

Murphy laughed, but it was not genuine in the slightest. He found nothing funny about this at all. His laughter was merely a mockery of Milo.

"So there's a shooting and the sheriff sits on his rear end until the smoke clears while three of my men get killed?"

"I reckon," Milo muttered.

This earned him a swift kick to the ribs.

"Tell me something," Murphy continued. "What good is having my brother be the sheriff when he won't even back my play?

For this, Milo had no answer.

"I finally get things set up to make my move and you prove to be worthless!"

These words hurt. It was so palpable that even Preston felt their sting. Milo knew his brother was right though. He had no business being a lawman. He didn't have the heart or the guts to face up to any real trouble. His position as sheriff was just for appearances anyway. It was agreed among the Coles that Milo would take the office because he was likable enough around town and he'd do as he was told.

"I let you down," Milo said barely above a whisper.

Murphy looked down at him. He was disgusted, but trying to move on to plan his next move.

"Get up."

Milo did as he was told while Murphy poured himself a drink of whiskey and sat down.

"What are you going to do to make up for it?" Murphy asked.

"I got my deputies bringing over the bodies," he replied. "Then we're going to arrest those Barkhouses."

"No."

"Huh?"

Milo was caught off guard by Murphy's reaction as he'd thought that this was a logical next step. The look Murphy shot him confirmed that this was not the case.

"I don't want you to do anything," Murphy instructed. "I've got to figure this out. I'm sure you'd screw it up anyways."

Like Milo, Preston understood that a mistake had been made, but couldn't quite comprehend the level of chastening that was being meted out. After all, Milo hadn't known that anything was going to happen.

Murphy sat quietly long enough that both Preston and Milo figured that it was time for them to leave. It was best to leave him along when he had such heavy issues on his mind. Besides, there were bodies to be buried.

***

At the Barkhouse home, Belle was a nervous wreck. She'd been enjoying the time spent with Claire and Luke, but couldn't stave off the feeling that something terrible was going to or had happened to Talmadge and the boys.

"I believe I hear something. Maybe it's them," she told Claire and Luke.

The unmistakable sound of the wheels on the buckboard turning over came into clear hearing. Belle rushed outside to see how they'd fared. When she saw Talmadge and Chauncey aboard the wagon with no accompanying horses, her heart sank.

"No!" she cried out as she hit her knees.

Luke and Claire rushed to her side, helping her to her feet as Augustus emerged from the barn. Talmadge steered the wagon up in front of the house and climbed down to comfort his wife. The entire family was crying as the dead bodies of Avery and Lake were viewed.

Once she was able to speak, Belle turned to Claire.

"Tell your daddy what you told me."

Talmadge looked at her curiously. Claire was still trying to compose herself, but choked back the tears long enough to say a couple of words.

"I'm pregnant."

# Chapter Sixteen

Giles Kayser's conscience was heavy. His son had been murdered by Murphy Cole's men just like Talmadge's. Although their cattle hadn't been killed or stolen, Simon's heart was in the right place. He was being loyal to his best friend even if it may not have been the wisest thing to do. It had cost him his life, but he went out a friend.

Giles knew that he'd be lying to himself if he said that he hadn't felt some resentment toward Talmadge for Simon's death. Deep down, he knew that there was nothing that could have been done in that situation. Talmadge hadn't known what those boys were going to do any more than he had. All the same, it was human nature.

He had decided now though that it was time to step up and do what Simon had done. It was time to be a true friend. He didn't know what he could do, but he would have to figure out something. He'd promised to help before when Talmadge had gone to the lawyer, but with Curtis' death, he'd once again fallen to the wayside.

After Lake and Avery had been laid to rest, he asked Talmadge to come with him so they could discuss what had happened and what they needed to do next. Talmadge obliged after being assured that Chauncey and Augustus would get their mother home safely.

The two patriarchs saddled up their horses and headed out to make a round where their cattle grazed, but mostly just to talk. They rode in silence for a while before Giles could find the words he wanted to say.

"I failed you, Tal."

Talmadge seemed a little surprised, but only looked over at his friend without saying a word.

"You needed my help and I was scared," Giles continued. "We hadn't had to do no fighting in so long and I reckon I lost my nerve."

Talmadge thought these words over and knew there was truth in them. He and Giles had fought side by side on multiple occasions but that had been years ago. They'd been peaceful people for a long time now.

"I understand," he said. "Finding myself back with a gun in my hand didn't feel right."

This was something that had been eating at Talmadge since this whole ordeal had begun and had only gotten worse since the shootout in town. After so much time of only using a gun as a tool to work cattle, using one to take a life brought about a great deal of inner conflict. It scared him just how willing his body was to go through those old motions. He was equally as scared that his boys had seemed to take to gun fighting so quickly and easily. He hadn't wanted this for them, but sometimes desperation gave a man no choice.

"I don't know what to do," Talmadge told Giles. "I know he's going to keep coming, I just don't know how."

They both knew that this was the case. They'd long had silent suspicions about Murphy Cole, but they'd now been proven true. People were dying left and right and it seemed like the only way out of this mess was straight through it. Neither the Barkhouses nor Kaysers could afford to run. Everything they had was tied up in their ranches.

Their meandering path led them into an old creek bed on the backside of the Barkhouse land where they found a half a dozen head of cattle that had clearly been shot. Talmadge was angry but not surprised.

"This still been happening a lot?" Giles asked.

"Every now and then we'll find a few," he replied. "Just enough to let us know he's still got his eyes on 'em."

Giles was sick to his stomach, but it had nothing to do with the dead animals lying before them. In fact, they were basically beyond the point of smelling. What nauseated him were the actions of a man that he had no real proof of being capable of such things. No, Murphy Cole had never been the friendliest of people, but this seemed like something you should see coming. They'd had no idea of what his plans were, but they were fully aware now.

Talmadge had the same feelings, only stronger. He was having to bury sons and he'd been forced to do things he'd hoped he'd never have to do again.

"I don't know how much longer I can hold on," Talmadge added. "I can't afford to run and can't leave home long enough to try and make a sale."

Giles tried to offer assistance that he knew Talmadge wouldn't take.

"What if I tried to sell some cattle for you? I can't afford to buy 'em myself, but I could probably find you a buyer."

Talmadge just shook his head as they rode on away from the slaughtered beeves.

"It wouldn't matter. If I leave, he won't quit. You'll be next. He wants everything and he's got the means to take it."

They both knew he was right. Giles had tried to put it out of his mind, but he knew that his family and operation were in just as much danger as Talmadge's. It was not a matter of if, but when, Cole would make his move. He was a determined man and only growing angrier. Although the Barkhouses had managed to fight back and do some damage, they were still fighting a losing battle.

"Me and my boys will back you," Giles said. "But they've never seen gun fighting and you know how long it's been since I have."

"I'd hate to ask you to do that," was Talmadge's response.

"Well," Giles replied. "He killed my boy too."

This was not something that the two of them wished to have in common. It was out of their control though. The weight of one man's greed fell upon their shoulders.

"I don't know how much longer Belle can hold up," Talmadge confessed. "I don't know how much more I can stand for that matter."

His throat tightened as he tried to choke back all the emotions that were flooding over him. It took a few moments before he was able to continue what he was saying.

"It ain't right having to bury your youngins'. And it's a shame you can't turn to the law."

Then it hit Giles like a ton of bricks. He had it!

"What about Aaron?"

This caused Talmadge to bring his horse to a sudden halt. He looked at Giles as if he'd just parted the Red Sea.

"You just might have the answer."

\*\*\*

The Aaron that Giles was speaking of was Aaron Claiborne, an old friend of theirs. Claiborne was a marshal in a town called Bloomfield, Arkansas about 20 miles southeast of Fort Smith. The pair met the lawman while acquiring cattle for their push north. Meanwhile, Claiborne was in Fort Smith bringing in a fugitive that had made the mistake of wandering through Bloomfield.

A small-time rancher himself, he took a little personal time to visit the stockyard to survey the current inventory. Here, Aaron became fast friends with Talmadge and Giles. The stock, however, was not as promising as the friendships.

With the promise of superior stock arriving imminently, the Barkhouses and Kaysers needed to wait around a few days to inspect them.

Being a single man who slept in the back of his jail, Aaron couldn't personally put a roof over their heads, but Bloomfield had a nice enough hotel and he could get them a friendly rate. They knew that they wouldn't find a better offer in Fort Smith and gladly accepted.

Their new friend was making quite the impression. It wouldn't be the only one he'd make in the coming days.

Talmadge and Giles, along with their families, had been in town for just two days when they would become involved in a volatile situation.

Two families, the Martins and Wrights, had lived in the area around Bloomfield since before it was a town. They'd had a longstanding feud based mostly on petty disagreements involving land and river access. There was plenty to go around, but as people are wont to do, family members from both sides let greed take over at times.

The latest and most intense conflict came about when Seth Wright had struck a particularly gamy stretch of river where he was running a trap line. Once word got out, jealousy reared its ugly head. Wade Martin, an avid trapper himself, encroached upon Seth's territory and took some of the spoils for himself. Having food taken off of his family's table was not something that set well with Seth Wright.

Seth confronted Wade while he was in the midst of retrieving a beaver from one of his sets. The two exchanged words and if the rumors were to be believed, Seth brandished a knife. This led to weeks of back-and-forth arguments and threats of physical harm. Catching Seth in the act of vandalizing some of his traps was the final straw for Wade. He promised harsh retaliation and it was time to make good on his word.

Seth, his two brothers, and a cousin knew that trouble was coming and retreated to a small shack owned by the family. They didn't want the women or children involved so they sought to keep them out of harm's way.

The morning of their second day in waiting brought trouble to the Wright men.

Their shack was nestled in a small opening maybe a hundred yards square in the middle of a mature oak grove. They'd used it in times past as a place to tan hides and occasionally make liquor. At this point it stood mostly useless.

Using the thick cover of the surrounding timber, Wade and his comrades slipped in unnoticed and opened fire on the shack and its unprepared occupants. Wade and his brother Stephen were shooting from behind with two others firing from one side. No one was hit during their volley, but the threat had definitely become a promise fulfilled. Now they just had to wait out the Wrights.

Others in the area, obviously aware of the less than friendly past between the two families, had been paying close attention to the recent rumblings. One man, a fur-trader by the name of Johnny Nantz who did business with both Seth and Wade, had been keeping a particularly keen eye on the situation. Dead sellers, after all, are useless. As soon as he knew about the Martins' plans and when they would be carried out, he brought it to the attention of the marshal.

"Marshal, marshal!" Nantz exclaimed as he burst into the jail. "You need to come with me!"

Startled by the sudden entrance of Nantz, Claiborne was in a state of confusion. He looked up from his desk, bewildered.

"What are you talking about, Johnny?"

Claiborne thought that he'd gone mad. He couldn't think of anything going on around town that could be so drastically important and he hadn't heard any shooting or the like.

"It's Wade Martin and some others," Johnny said. "They've gone after the Wrights and they're armed to the teeth!"

This made sense. Like everyone else, the marshal had heard about the newest round of disagreements between the long-feuding families but had hoped it would blow over without his intervention. That would not be the case.

"Where are they?" he asked as he jumped up from his chair and threw his gun belt around his waist.

"Seth and them are holed up in a little shack east of Long's Pass," Johnny replied.

"Can you take me there?"

"Sure can."

And with that, they were off. Claiborne and Nantz ran outside, mounted up, and swiftly headed out of town for the Wrights' hideout. Across the street from the jail stood the hotel, where Giles and Talmadge stood out front watching the scene unfold.

"What do you suppose that's about?" asked Giles.

"I don't know. Seems mighty serious though."

As they neared the cutoff that would take them to the shack where the Wrights were unknowingly in a standoff with the Martins, Aaron and Johnny heard the unmistakable sound of gunfire.

"Sounds like we might be too late," Johnny remarked as he spurred his horse to move on faster.

"Easy now," Aaron instructed. "We don't want to go riding into no bullet."

Worried as he was about the prospect of someone dying in this exchange, Johnny certainly knew he didn't want it to be him. The pair slowed back, and when they could see the edge of the clearing, dismounted and led their horses carefully ahead.

By now, the air, though thick with the aroma of gunpowder, was free of the sound of shots being fired. Almost to the edge of the clearing, Aaron tied his horse off to a tree branch and eased his pistol from its holster.

"Hold steady here for the time being," he whispered to Johnny.

Johnny nodded and the marshal cleared his throat loudly to alert the others to his presence.

"It's Marshal Claiborne, gentlemen. Don't shoot!" he announced loudly.

He surveyed the area once more before stepping out into the open.

"Wade Martin, I know you're here. You too, Seth Wright."

Not knowing who else or how many may be around, Aaron played it carefully. He hoped that by calling them by name, he could establish a rapport with them that would serve to deescalate the situation.

"Yea marshal, we're in here," a voice cried out from within the weathered little bunker. "They're shooting at us!"

It had to be Seth.

"Are any of you hit?"

"No!"

"Good, that's good," replied the marshal, relieved.

At least he knew that no real harm had been done. Maybe they could all get out of there with only the holes they'd brought with them.

"Now, Wade," the marshal called out in search of a response.

He'd entered the clearing angling toward the southwest corner of the shack and couldn't see any of the Martins. Wade and Stephen were behind the shack, north, and their cohorts were on the eastern side. For several agonizing seconds there was no response. Aaron now worried that they had fled the scene.

"Yea?" Wade's answer finally came.

That was a relief.

"What's this all about, Wade?" the marshal asked.

Wade was hostile.

"Caught him stealing from my trap line and boogering up my damn traps!"

"Traps you set on a line I already had claim to!" Seth fired right back.

Aaron knew that this had the potential to get real ugly, real quick. Seth and Wade were continuing to mouth off at one another and the others were starting to chime in. He had to do something.

"Hold on a minute!" he yelled.

When they failed to notice him, Aaron fired a single round into the air. This got him the attention he desired. Everyone was on high alert, but realizing it was the marshal that had fired, they calmed a bit. Side-stepping gently toward the front of the house, he tried to diffuse the situation.

"This ain't worth killing each other over," he told them. "A few beavers, maybe a muskrat or otter."

Seth wasn't satisfied with this notion.

"He's taking food off my family's table!" he hollered.

"There's more than enough to go around and then some," Wade rebutted.

"Then go find your own!"

Aaron had no idea who was in the right or wrong here for sure and he didn't care. Right now his only job was to keep everyone from getting killed and figure out the rest later.

"Fellas!" he interrupted. "Let's not forget you've both got families. Killing or maiming each other don't do nobody any favors."

Even though they were angry and willing to shed blood, neither party was eager to be the one whose blood was spilled. Both were mulling over their options.

"And just what do you propose we do, Marshal?" Wade asked.

Now it was up to Aaron to figure out what his proposal should be.

"Let's try to settle this without guns. Nobody needs to die here."

This seemed to appeal to both sides.

"I've got Johnny Nantz here with me," he continued. "He'll be witness that you're all handled fair."

Johnny being there was an asset since Seth and Wade both considered him to be a friend. Aaron could use all the help he could get.

"Seth, I want you and whoever's in there to toss your guns out that little window next to the door," the marshal instructed.

Johnny now stood at his side, ready to assist in any way possible. The Wrights had begun to drop their guns outside like Aaron had requested. Several pistols and a couple of rifles now laid on the ground.

"Alright Wade, y'all come around and drop your guns by me."

Slowly, the four of them came from around the house. A harsh glance from Wade in his adversaries' direction worried Aaron, but nothing came of it. He and the others came over and laid their guns down without a hiccup.

"Now step over there," he said as he motioned to his right.

Once they'd obliged and he felt sure that everyone was unarmed, Aaron invited the Wrights to step outside. One by one, they slowly exited the shack and stepped away from their guns. Seth hovered in the doorway a second too long and it alarmed Aaron. There was nothing he could do though. Seth snatched a rifle from behind the door and blasted away at Wade. Two bullets rapidly found their mark and killed him dead.

Everyone was in shock, even the other Wrights who didn't seem to know that this was going to occur. Wade's family looked down at him and then back to Aaron. They felt that they'd been set up for an ambush. Betrayal was the first thing that came to mind. Aaron knew right away that this was the most likely outcome. He quickly turned his gun on Seth.

"Drop it!" he demanded.

Seth didn't appear to have it out for any others as he immediately dropped the rifle.

"Keep your gun on them, Johnny," he said in reference to the Martins as he approached Seth and his family.

Forcefully, he grabbed Seth by the ear and snatched him in the direction of where he and Johnny came from, his pistol still in hand.

"Where's your horse?" Aaron growled.

"We left 'em home."

Aaron turned back to Johnny.

"Can he double with you?"

Johnny nodded.

"Where you think you're taking him?" Stephen asked.

With a firm grip still on the killer's ear, Aaron stared Stephen down.

"I'm taking him to jail. He just murdered a man and he'll stand trial. I'm the law and that's how it'll be done."

Stephen wanted to buck this, but he thought better of it. It was obvious that the marshal was not to be tested.

A short while later, a small convoy came into town with Johnny out front. Riding with him was Seth Wright, his hands tied, and Aaron following behind with his pistol laying across his saddle. As they approached the jail, the Martins followed at a distance with Wade's dead body draped across his horse.

Out front of the jail stood a welcome surprise. Talmadge and Giles awaited Aaron, both with their guns around their waists. Their intuition that something was awry had been spot on.

"Boy am I glad to see y'all," Aaron remarked as he got down from his horse.

"Trouble coming I see," Giles said as he looked back up the street.

"Afraid so. Come on inside."

After helping Seth down from Johnny's horse, Aaron looked to Johnny.

"You best ride on, Johnny. Don't want you having trouble with friends."

"Thank you," Johnny said and quickly rode on.

Inside, Aaron secured Seth in a cell and gave his new friends a crash course in the history of the Wright-Martin feud. He wondered what he'd done in the past to be burdened with its most serious episode. A voice from outside broke his concentration.

"Get out here, Marshal!" screamed Doug Martin, a cousin of Wade's who had been present for the ruckus.

"Here we go," the marshal muttered under his breath as he stepped out of the door with Talmadge and Giles in tow.

He'd never had a need for deputies, but he now had two unofficial ones standing abreast of him on the jail's small porch.

Doug was more bold than his cousin Stephen had been. Both of them had the mouth, but Doug seemed more willing to act.

"We want him, Marshal," he said plainly.

"Well you ain't getting him."

Doug smiled devilishly as he cocked the hammer on the rifle he held.

"You sure you want to do that?" Aaron asked as he pulled back the hammer on his own gun.

Just then it hit Talmadge. He was certain that Aaron had been tailed into town by three men, but only two stood before them. Quickly, he snuck a glance through the front door and noticed a beam of light that hadn't been there previously.

"Hold them," Talmadge instructed as he made his move.

He spun on his heels and rushed inside just in time to see Stephen step into the room with a pistol drawn. Stephen made for Seth's cell and Talmadge yelled at him.

"There won't be none of that!"

Caught off guard, Stephen froze momentarily. Seth dove under the bunk in his cell to take cover. Talmadge held his aim on Stephen, who made a fatal mistake. He turned his gun on Talmadge and was met with two bullets to the sternum, knocking him against the wall.

As soon as the shooting commenced inside, Doug tried to swing his rifle around on the marshal, but he was too slow. He didn't know who'd shot first, but he knew he had to shoot next. He was right, but too bad for him, a long gun in close quarters can be a detriment. Aaron had put a bullet in his brain before the rifle was even remotely pointed in his direction.

Not paying any mind to Giles, the fourth Martin had his eyes set on Aaron too. Giles fired and struck him in the left arm, spinning him out into the street. Upon recognizing the source of his affliction, he aimed for Giles, but missed wildly amid a hail of fire from both Giles and Aaron.

Stephen scooted himself up against the wall inside as best he could, but kept sliding down, leaving a smear of blood behind him. Finally, after a handful of unsuccessful attempts, he just gave up. Within a minute he'd breathed his last.

All four of the Martins who had pursued the Wrights were now dead. Aaron knew that it may not set well with some, but he knew he'd done the right thing all along. He also knew that he was grateful to have had Talmadge and Giles by his side for the bloody affair.

The Barkhouse and Kayser families stayed around long enough to purchase some of the new, superior stock from Fort Smith. Despite Aaron's half-joking attempts at securing them as deputies, Talmadge and Giles decided it was time to move on with their families and settle down. They'd fought enough in the war and the killing they'd done backing Aaron was simply a favor to a friend. Of course, Aaron understood and stood ready to return their favor at a moment's notice.

He often reminded them of such in the letters they'd shared over the years. Those letters had become less and less frequent and Aaron had only made it up to see them twice in all these years for he was a busy man. Still, the bond these three men was vault-strong and bound in blood.

As it turned out, Aaron wouldn't be long for Bloomfield either. Just a few months after the incident with the Wrights and Martins, he took an offer to move to Oklahoma and become a territorial marshal. The work was wilder and more suited to him than watching over a town. He worked that job for a few years before moving on to his current position: United States Marshal.

# Chapter Seventeen

A few things had actually gone in the Barkhouses' favor recently. There'd been no attacks from Cole for a while, not even on their cattle. Talmadge knew that this luck wouldn't hold, but he hoped that it would remain that way until he could hear from Aaron.

As it just so happened, Aaron came into his office only a couple of days after the letter from Talmadge detailing their troubles arrived. There was no hesitation on his part; he was ready to go the next morning without notifying any superiors. This matter was personal and would be handled in such a way.

Though not a great fan of trains, Aaron decided it was the fastest route to Langston. If even half of what Talmadge had written was true, and he knew it all was, his friends were in dire straits.

With their good timing and the convenience of rail travel, Aaron arrived in Langston just over a month after the letter written to him had left. He didn't bother to respond, opting to rather to get to where he was needed as quickly as possible.

Aaron's arrival was a happy one until the solemnity of the situation hit them all. Everyone from both families were glad to see him and he was glad to see them, even if under difficult circumstances. Regardless of all the catching up they had to do, Aaron was ready to get down to the business at hand.

"If this Cole fella is as nasty as y'all say he is, we need to move quick," he told them. "It'll probably get ugly.

"Well, it ain't been too pretty so far," Talmadge remarked.

They'd all, except for Mary and Martha who they'd deemed too young to hear such things, gathered to discuss how to best go about settling this conflict.

"I'm more than glad to help," Aaron continued. "But we're going to have to do it my way."

He'd get no argument there.

They all trusted him implicitly, knowing that he knew better how to squash such problems than they did. It was not a matter that he took lightly, mulling it over his whole trip there. He knew that with all the blood that had been spilled already, a peaceful resolution was not likely. Still, he wanted to try.

"So what are we gonna do?" Belle asked.

She was so heartbroken at this point that she'd try anything.

"Y'all are gonna have to agree to let what happened in the past stay there if it can."

"How?" was Talmadge's question.

He had faith in Aaron, but this just didn't seem feasible. Although he didn't have as much riding on this proposition as his friend, Giles wondered the same thing.

"I'm gonna give him an ultimatum," Aaron said. "If he'll drop the whole mess, you will too."

"Well I doubt he does that," Giles threw in.

"So do I," Aaron agreed. "But I'll give him that choice."

Now they were skeptical. Just what kind of plan was this? There was no way that Murphy Cole was just going to roll over. He'd proven to them what he wanted and to what lengths he would go to get just that.

"Then what's the flip side of that coin?" Talmadge asked.

"We'll start killing on sight without prejudice any man that rides for him."

This was beginning to sound like a plan they could get on board with. The women were horrified at the prospect of more killing, but understood that it was likely coming one way or another.

"Well?" asked Aaron.

The Barkhouses and Kaysers all shared silent, knowing glances and Talmadge gave a subtle nod. This was all Aaron needed.

\*\*\*

There was nothing physically remarkable about U.S. Marshal Aaron Claiborne. To say he was five and a half feet tall might have been a slight exaggeration. His build was thin other than a slight belly that had begun to hang on him in the last few years. He had dull gray eyes and wore an unkempt beard most of the time. Even his clothes were plain, including the faded ankle-length duster he wore. This garment was not an item worn as a fashion statement, but one of practicality for a man who spent a lot of time on horseback.

Claiborne hardly garnered any looks as he walked down Langston's main street and approached the jail. He traipsed right on in unnoticed until he was through the door.

Inside, Murphy Cole sat behind his brother's desk with his feet propped up on the desk, a position very familiar to the furniture. His son Preston and Jasper Maxwell flanked him on either side.

"Can I help you?" Murphy asked Aaron.

The marshal took a moment to inspect the scene. He noticed the star on Jasper's chest, but doubted he was the law around there considering he wasn't the man seated at the big desk.

"I hope so," Aaron replied. "I'm looking for Milo Cole. I understand he's the sheriff around here."

"He is. But he's out on business."

This was true. Milo was out on business, but it had nothing to do with his office. He, along with his deputies

Warren Clement and Roger Nelson, was gone to hire guns for Murphy.

"You must be his deputy," Aaron said, turning his attention to Jasper.

"Yes sir," he said quietly.

"And I'm his brother," Murphy chimed in.

The bravado with which Murphy offered this information told Aaron that this was likely the man he was really looking for.

"You wouldn't be Murphy, would you?" he asked wryly.

"Uh, yeah," Murphy said, surprised that this man knew his name.

Murphy had always had a high opinion of himself, but he had no idea who this stranger was or why he knew his name.

"Well that's even better then," Aaron said enthusiastically. "You're my real reason for being here. Just figured a lawman would be easier to find."

Now Murphy was intrigued. He swung his legs down from the desk and stood up, extending a hand to Aaron.

"Have a seat Mr..."

"Aaron Claiborne."

"Mr. Claiborne."

"Aaron will do," the marshal said as he shook the big rancher's hand.

The pair took a seat as Preston and Jasper stood up a little straighter, watching intently. Murphy quickly ran the name Aaron Claiborne through his mind, trying to figure out if it had any significance to him. He couldn't think of anything and decided to speak for fear of seeming ignorant by sitting quietly in thought.

"So Aaron," he began. "What business does a man I don't know have with me?"

"It's simple, really," Aaron said without emotion. "I believe we have a mutual acquaintance."

"And who might that be?"

"Talmadge Barkhouse."

If Murphy wanted to play it cool, he couldn't. His face told on him. His brow furrowed and his jaw twitched a little. These movements were not lost on Aaron. He'd been reading men and their reactions for a long time. It was a job requirement.

Murphy was left more perplexed now that he knew why Aaron was there than he was when he had no clue who he was. Who could this man possibly be? He had a cool way of talking, and now that Murphy thought of it, a dangerous air about him. Maybe he was a gunman. Did he plan to kill him right here? Surely Talmadge hadn't grown that bold.

"What about him?" he asked Aaron, trying to regain the confidence they both knew he had lost.

Aaron was the total opposite of Murphy at this point. He was cool, calm, and collected. He knew he would get the upper hand quickly just by mentioning Talmadge's name.

"He happens to be a friend of mine."

Aaron had made the decision not to include Giles in this conversation unless necessary. As far as Murphy knew, his only involvement was Simon being with Asa when he went to steal back the cattle. If everything worked out for the best, it would remain that way.

"From what I understand," Aaron continued. "You two have had some issues over the last several months."

"I don't know what you're talking about."

Aaron grinned. He knew Murphy was lying just as well as the other men in the room knew he was lying.

"Oh, I believe you do," was his reply.

Murphy figured there was no point in lying now, not completely anyhow. Aaron obviously knew what was going on. Now he'd get Murphy's convoluted version of the truth.

"Talmadge accused me of stealing his cattle," he offered. "Or his boy did."

"Did you?"

"I said accused."

His words were harsh now. Not being a long-tempered man under any circumstances, Murphy was even less patient and quick to anger when dealing with people he didn't like. He didn't like Talmadge Barkhouse, and by association, he didn't like Aaron Claiborne.

"About Talmadge's boy?" Aaron prodded.

Murphy took his time in answering. He reached in his shirt pocket and extracted one of his cigars. He planned to take over this conversation and let Aaron know just how unimportant him or any of the Barkhouses were to him. Finally, he spoke.

"Him and one of Giles Kayser's boys came to my ranch accusing me of stealing cattle and trying to rustle some of mine."

Aaron acted as if Giles' name meant nothing to him. "And you killed 'em?

Murphy was ill, but keeping his cool. He was a master manipulator and he was doing his best to apply his craft. Unfortunately for him, Aaron's mind was made up before he ever walked in the door. He wasn't there to be manipulated.

"I don't know where you're from mister..." Murphy trailed off, looking for an answer.

"Arkansas originally."

"I don't know about in Arkansas, but in Montana we give rustlers what they deserve."

Aaron knew he wasn't going to get any straight answers, but he wanted to push just a little further.

"How 'bout the black fella that worked for you?"

"Curtis?"

"Yea. He try to rustle your cattle too?"

Now Murphy was almost at his breaking point. His already thin patience was threadbare now.

"State your business," he demanded. "I'm tired of you beating around the bush.

Maybe Aaron had gone a little too far, but he didn't care. He was almost positive that Murphy wouldn't accept his proposition and he didn't like the man anyhow. Getting under his skin was just a bonus. It wouldn't bother him one bit if Murphy or either of the other two tried to draw on him right now. In fact, he'd welcome it.

"You see," Aaron began. "Talmadge wanted me to make you an offer."

"Oh yeah?" Murphy laughed.

"Yeah. He's willing to let bygones be bygones if you will."

Murphy was surprised to hear this. It made him more confident though. If Talmadge was this desperate after all that had been done to his family, he had to be close to giving up. There was no way Murphy would accept, but he wanted to amuse himself.

"You know, he ain't the only one's been hurt here. I've lost men too."

"I'm aware. They're tired of hurting. Figured you might be too."

What most likely didn't register for the Barkhouses or Aaron was the fact that Murphy wasn't hurt, he was angry. He couldn't care less about the lives of those men, regardless of how loyal they had been to him. He only cared that their absence made him weaker.

"How would that work exactly?" Murphy asked. "How could I trust him to hold up his end of the deal?"

"I'd keep an eye on things for a while."

Murphy couldn't help but laugh.

"You? How could you be impartial?"

"Talmadge has been a real good friend to me. There's nothing I'd love to do more than to make sure his family is safe. No way I can guarantee that if I let this fighting go on."

This made a lot of sense to Murphy, but he still had no plans of even considering it. He knew he had gun hands on the way and Talmadge was vulnerable. This new arrival wouldn't hinder his plans.

"And suppose I don't accept this truce?" Murphy asked nonchalantly.

"Then that's where I really come in."

Murphy sat up as straight as he could possibly get in his chair.

"And how's that?"

Aaron didn't crack a smile and the inflection of his voice didn't change in the slightest. What he said was stated straightforward, almost coldly.

"I'm gonna give you until noon tomorrow to make your decision. If you accept the offer, fine. If you don't, I start killing on sight. You or any man rides for you dies if he shows his face."

Hell flew into Murphy Cole. He couldn't believe this cocky little man had the nerve to walk in here and speak to him like that. He flew to his feet and stood there brooding, towering over Aaron. His attempt to intimidate the smaller man with his sheer size was a waste. Aaron knew he was smaller than most and it didn't bother him.

"Who the hell do you think you are?" Murphy screamed. "You don't get to come into my town and threaten me you little bastard!"

Preston and Jasper looked on with bated breath, wondering what Aaron might say. Both of them could see this erupting soon.

"It ain't no threat. You see that?" he asked as he peeled his duster back, revealing the badge pinned to his chest. "It says United States Marshal. Means I can do whatever I damn well please."

No one saw this coming. The sudden appearance of another badge in Langston flabbergasted Murphy. He had no idea that Talmadge had these kinds of connections. He wasn't sure how lethal this marshal was, but he certainly seemed to be serious.

Murphy's broad shoulders slouched as he watched Aaron rise from his chair. He wanted to act, but he wasn't sure what to do, if anything at this moment.

"Noon, tomorrow," the marshal told him as he prepared to leave. "I'll be here."

Not trusting them to not shoot him in the back, Aaron slipped out of the door without ever taking his eyes off of the three men.

Preston and Jasper both had a plethora of questions they wanted to ask, but neither of them dared to say a word.

\*\*\*

That night, Murphy had his brothers and every man in his command over for a meal and meeting to address what had been presented to them earlier that day. Of course, Montgomery was not invited.

While he had his doubts earlier considering the ferociousness of the marshal, Murphy now sat at the head of his table with a newfound confidence. There was still a good number of men at his disposal: four of his own remaining men, his son, three brothers, and his brother's three deputies. Furthermore, he was emboldened by Milo's hiring of Toby Wheeler, Jose Amaro, and Harry Bradshaw, three gunmen he was assured were of the highest regard in their profession.

Even if the Kaysers helped the Barkhouses, that still gave them a distinct advantage of 15 men to 7, including Claiborne. The Kaysers lending them a hand seemed doubtful as Murphy hadn't heard a peep from them since their son had been killed. Even better, that would make only 4 men to kill. With those odds, he might not even lose a man.

As they sopped their plates clean and concluded their meeting, Murphy's instructions were clear.

"Gene, I want you and Preston to go tomorrow," he said. "Claiborne said he'd be at the jail at noon so y'all show up about quarter after, maybe 12:30."

"Yes sir," the two of them said in unison.

"You look that son of a bitch in his eyes and tell him I said no. Nothing else, just flat no."

They both nodded as Murphy turned his attention to Milo.

"I want you in the jail ready to be their backup. If any shooting starts, come running. The rest of y'all be on standby for my next orders."

With everyone informed of what was expected of them, Murphy got up from the table and headed to the den for his nightly whiskey and smoke.

# Chapter Eighteen

Aaron Claiborne was aboard his horse and ready to leave for town when Talmadge approached him from the barn.

"Sure you don't want us to ride with you?" he asked.

"I'm sure," Aaron told him. "If you want any shot at peace, I'd best go alone."

Talmadge sort of nodded his head, then dropped it and looked at his shuffling boots.

"That is what you want, ain't it?" asked Aaron, sensing the unsurety. "'Cause if not, we'll gather Giles and his boys and ride on Cole's house right now."

They both laughed at this idea. It was stated in jest, but Aaron could just as well be serious about it and Talmadge knew it. The chances of Murphy Cole ever taking this offer were slim to none and Talmadge was tempted to just start shooting. This wasn't in his nature though.

"I reckon you better ride alone."

Aaron nodded and started his horse, but was stopped.

"Just one more thing," Talmadge said. "There's someone I want you to stop and see before you go to the jail."

"Yea? Who's that?"

*** 

Reverend Montgomery Cole was at quiet prayer in his church as he often was at the pre-noon hour when he heard heavy footsteps approaching the front doors.

One of the double doors was opened, casting a bright ray of light in. The preacher sat at the end of the front, right pew looking in with his head bowed, eyes closed, and grasping his Bible in both hands.

"Come on in, brother," he said without turning to see who had entered.

"I ain't your brother," Aaron Claiborne replied.

"Well maybe not in the earthly sense," was the reverend's response.

By now, Montgomery stood in the middle of the aisle between the pews. With the door now closed, he could take a good look at his guest.

"You seemed awfully happy to greet a stranger," Aaron remarked. "And suppose I'd been a lady you'd greeted in such a way."

There was no ill will in Claiborne's words and the preacher could tell it. Despite his sometimes harsh demeanor, the marshal could be quite jovial once you'd taken time to scratch the surface. This facade came in quite handy in his line of work, but he felt no need to display it with a man of the Lord that he'd heard nothing but good about.

"Well mister, the only woman I ever knew that walked that hard was my mama when she was after one of us boys. And you're not my mama."

"Nor your brother," Aaron replied with a sly grin.

Montgomery didn't know where this conversation was headed, but if it could possibly lead to a saved soul, he was more than happy to partake.

"There's still time for that," was his own clever response.

Both men smiled at this and Montgomery extended his hand as the pair neared each other. Aaron accepted it without hesitation. This was definitely a different breed of Cole and it didn't take long to figure out.

"Reverend Montgomery Cole, but most people call me Preacher or Monty."

"U.S. Marshal Aaron Claiborne."

A knowing look overtook Monty's face, confirming to Aaron that his name was not new to the reverend's ears.

"So you're the lawman I heard about."

"From your brother?"

Another look from Monty confused Aaron.

"No, but word finds its way around. Murphy's not my biggest fan," he said.

"I'm guessing that makes two of us," Aaron told him.

Neither man had bothered to take a seat.

"So what brings you here?" asked Monty.

"A man that thinks a lot of you actually."

"And who might that be?"

"Talmadge Barkhouse."

It only took a moment for things to click for Monty. He knew well the war that his brother had waged on Talmadge and his family. Talmadge was not an easy man to anger, but Murphy was relentless. It made a lot of sense for him to bring in some help. Monty could see this getting ugly in a hurry.

"I see," was all he could muster.

Aaron knew that this was putting Monty in an undesirable situation and why Talmadge had wanted him to stop by the church.

"I'm backing Talmadge against your brother," Aaron said solemnly. "He wanted me to extend you the courtesy of letting you know before anything happens."

The preacher just nodded. He understood why things had to be this way, but hoped it wouldn't get to this point.

"It's in Murphy's hands now," Aaron continued. "But I don't see any way around it getting ugly."

"Neither do I," Monty agreed sadly.

Knowing that even a man of the cloth felt the same way he did about the impending decision took away what little sliver of hope he had for avoiding violence. He was more than willing to go with that, but there was something else he needed to know.

"Where do you stand in this?" he asked Monty.

"I stand with the Lord, Mr. Claiborne. He hasn't failed me yet."

This response was comforting for Aaron. He had no desire to go against a preacher, especially one that was so likable.

"Well that's good to hear."

"You do what you feel you must marshal and so will I," Monty assured him. "As long as you don't find yourself opposite God, we'll have no issue. I swore an oath to Him that goes beyond any mortal man."

Aaron could tell that this was a genuine response and he appreciated it. There was no doubt in his mind that Talmadge and Giles were wise to think so highly of their preacher.

"Fair enough," Aaron offered with his hand extended.

Monty took his hand and they shook.

"All goes well," the marshal added. "This might be the last time we ever see each other."

"Regardless of how things go with my brother, there's much more we could talk about," said Monty as he tapped his Bible.

"Maybe," Aaron laughed.

With that, Aaron turned on his heels and left. His entire disposition changed as he exited the doors of the church. The hard-nosed marshal was back.

He untied his horse and walked him down the street in the direction of the jail, not bothering to climb aboard. Knowing who he was now, several people eyed him as he walked. He studied every inch of his surroundings, looking out for possible assassins, but saw nothing out of place. Maybe Murphy Cole had underestimated him, or perhaps he planned to take the deal. One could hope.

Upon his arrival at the jail, Claiborne tied up his horse around the side and took a look into the jail. What he saw was Milo Cole in the same relaxed position he'd found Murphy the day before. Milo appeared to be asleep though, and without company. He certainly didn't look like a man who was expecting trouble nor did he look like a messenger.

Rather than waking the sheriff, the marshal decided to have a seat in one of the chairs on the jail's small porch. It occurred to him that this jail was better suited for socializing than what it should be for. This was an assumption he was correct in.

Claiborne didn't bother to remove his duster as he sat down. To some, this long coat may appear to be a hindrance in a seated position, but he wore it so often, it just seemed natural to him. He pulled his timepiece out of his pocket and gave it a look. It was 11:57. He didn't expect punctuality from his counterparts and he wouldn't get it.

That was alright though. Claiborne had patience in spades when the situation called for it. In a little while, two men who looked like they meant business exited the saloon down the street and headed his way. He took another look at his watch once he knew for sure these men were coming to see him; it was 12:25.

Claiborne stood from his seat and stepped to the edge of the porch, tucking his hands into the front of his britches.

"I assume you're looking for me?" he asked.

"You Claiborne?" asked Gene Cook.

"I am," he nodded. "Y'all Murphy Cole's men?"

Gene and Preston looked at each other and shared a laugh. To say they were Murphy Cole's men was a drastic understatement.

"That's right," Cook said cockily. "I'm Gene Cook and this here is Preston Cole."

Claiborne was surprised that a Cole was present for this exchange.

"You Murphy's boy?" Claiborne asked Preston.

"Sure am," he answered proudly.

This was enough small talk for the marshal. He was ready to get down to business.

"Now that we're all acquainted," he said. "What'd your boss man say?"

"No," Cook replied confidently.

"Just no?"

Claiborne wasn't surprised that his offer wasn't being accepted, but he'd expected more than a single word answer.

"That's right," Preston Cole interjected.

Having a powerful father made the young man much bolder than he had any right to be. His mettle was about to be put to the test.

Claiborne eased his right hand out of his waistband and slipped his duster back behind the handle of his revolver. One look at the weathered grip of Claiborne's single action cavalry model Colt told Gene Cook that both he and his boss had both been sorely mistaken in underestimating this marshal. Anyone with Cook's background knew that a gun handle didn't show that kind of wear without plenty of use.

His instincts set him into motion, but Claiborne was quicker, much quicker. Just as Cook's hand made contact with the butt of his pistol, the marshal cleared leather and obtained his target in one slick motion. The bullet found its mark just over Cook's right eyebrow and a slow trickle of blood oozed from the entry wound. His face lost all expression as he stumbled back a half step before collapsing to the ground, dead.

In a fraction of a second and without hesitation, Claiborne turned his attention to Preston, Murphy Cole's only son. It was a shame that his father had sent him there to die.

Claiborne smoothly cycled the cylinder of his Colt with a quick flip of his thumb as if he'd done it a thousand times. Maybe he had.

The young man was caught off guard and fumbled clumsily as he reached for his own revolver. He was rattled by the gunfire. It was so sudden, so close. His unfamiliarity with this kind of situation killed him. That and U.S. Marshal Aaron Claiborne.

Claiborne fired again. This bullet drilled Preston just above his upper lip and sent his shattered teeth flying to the back of his head. He hit the dusty street with a ground-shaking thud as a pained groan escaped his mouth. He was in a great deal of agony, but his body wouldn't have worked even if he could have thought to try to move it.

Coolly, Claiborne stepped off the porch of the jail onto the street between the bodies that lay fallen. He worked the hammer one more time and planted a finishing shot in the forehead of Preston Cole.

In just a matter of moments, Claiborne had laid waste to two men before either one had even had time to so much as draw their pistol. He was a dangerous man and he had a badge.

For the first time, his left hand moved from its place in his waistband. Claiborne flipped open the loading gate of his cylinder and casually ejected his three spent cartridge hulls. Just as nonchalantly, he plucked three new rounds from his gun belt to replace them.

Behind him he heard the door of the jail swing open. Claiborne spun around on his heels to face Milo, who had stumbled out onto the porch. Both his eyes and mouth flew open when he saw the two men lying dead on the ground with the marshal standing over them. This was not what he'd expected at all.

"Howdy," Claiborne offered wryly with a tip of his hat.

Feeling no immediate threat, he holstered his gun and waited for a reply. Milo only stared in disbelief. At Claiborne, then down at Gene and Preston, then back to Claiborne.

"Wha... what's the meaning of this?" Milo stammered.

He knew that Murphy said this marshal had made bold claims, but he couldn't believe it now that he was seeing the results firsthand.

"You're Milo, Murphy's brother right?" Claiborne asked. "The sheriff."

Still, Milo only looked toward him blankly.

"Right?" Claiborne asked again.

Milo was finally able to make his mind and mouth work together to utter a thought in the marshal's direction.

"Uh, yeah," he said. "But what's all this about?"

"Well you're Murphy's brother so you should know."

"How's that?"

By now, several people had spilled out onto the street and were looking on at the results of the carnage that had taken place. Nobody dared come closer though. Danger and tension filled the air.

"Are you aware that your brother and I spoke yesterday afternoon?" Claiborne questioned. "Right there in your jail."

Milo glanced over his shoulder then back at Claiborne. He took a quick look around at the onlookers but again back to Claiborne.

Milo nodded.

"Yeah, we talked about it last night."

"And?" Claiborne stared at him inquisitively. "What'd he say?"

"Said you offered him sort of deal but he weren't gonna take it."

"He tell you what it meant if he turned down my offer?"

"Supposedly you were going to kill any of his men you saw on sight" Milo replied.

"That's right," Claiborne returned.

Both men looked down at the slain bodies still lying where they fell, and then back up at one another.

"I'm just getting started. And it looks like you're next," he added.

Milo's eyes darted back and forth nervously as he tried to decide his next move. He glanced around at the onlookers as if he may somehow find the answer he was looking for on one of their faces. After several tense moments, he spoke.

"This has nothing to do with me. I don't want any part in it."

He was quickly backtracking on what he'd told his brother he'd do. He couldn't think of any place worse to be at this moment.

"That's too bad. Your brother already tied you up in it," Claiborne replied.

Milo only shook his head.

"No."

He turned back toward the door of the jail. As he did, Claiborne redrew his revolver from his holster and pointed it in Milo's direction. Milo's hand was nearly touching the doorknob when the sound of a hammer cocking stopped him in his tracks. He looked back over his shoulder at the marshal but didn't turn around.

"You wouldn't shoot me in the back. You're a lawman for Christ's sake."

"You willing to bet your life on it?" Claiborne fired back.

Milo grabbed for the knob and gripped it.

"In the back or I'll give you a fair shot."

Again the sheriff looked back over his shoulder at his adversary. This time though, he let go of the doorknob and turned to face Claiborne.

"I guess I don't have much of a choice then," he said less than confidently.

"Guess not."

Understanding that he must make his move, Milo stepped down off of the porch and into street. The spectators withdrew from the street, either under the eaves of the buildings or indoors.

The two men stared at each other coldly. Claiborne was, without question, the calmer of the two. He dropped his hand down by his side and eased the hammer forward on his gun, and with only his thumb and first finger, slipped it back into his holster. With the palm of his hand, he pushed it down deeper, securing it and guaranteeing a fair shake for Milo.

Milo eased his hand down toward his holster and unsnapped his guard. He and Claiborne couldn't have been more than seven or eight paces from each other. His heart pounded as he studied the marshal, searching for an opportunity to draw. Claiborne gently moved his hand away from his gun, but it hovered nearby. On the main street of Langston, these two lawmen studied each other for a few more agonizing seconds.

Finally, Claiborne dropped his empty right hand by his side. Just as it reached its lowest point, Milo grabbed for the butt of his pistol. He was a hair faster than his nephew or Gene Cook but still not fast enough. Claiborne's own gun flashed from his holster and he brought his arm up hurriedly. The first shot sounded out and smacked Milo in his right collarbone. This halted his upward swing and he fired a shot into the ground near Claiborne's feet. Another bullet crashed into Milo's sternum and he wobbled back a step before stumbling forward.

A final shot blew out a major artery in the sheriff's neck and blood gushed from it. They were so close together by then that his neck was burnt from the muzzle blast. The blood flow slowed to a mere spurt as Claiborne watched in amazement that his victim hadn't left his feet. Milo's hand fell open and he dropped his gun as he fell flat on his face, landing on Claiborne's boots. Claiborne looked down and noticed for the first time that the front of his shirt and duster were splattered with Milo's blood.

After being a bit mesmerized by the blood for a brief moment, he turned to face the people who had witnessed the slaughtering. His experiences in such situations told him it was time to go. The message had been sent loud and clear: three of Murphy Cole's men lay dead in the street, including one of his brothers and his only son. Sooner or later, hanging around would lead to the odds turning against him.

Without bothering to reload his gun, Claiborne quickly holstered it and fetched his horse. He untied the stud and set off at a trot back up the street. The horse had barely set his pace when Marvin Cole stepped out of his store and into the street with a Winchester rifle in his hands, having been made aware of who was involved in the shooting going on in the street. As he brought the rifle to his shoulder, everyone who remained in the street dove for cover and Claiborne made his move. He cut the horse directly to his left just as Marvin's first bullet left the barrel. It whizzed through the air precisely where Claiborne had just been.

The horse and its rider ducked in between two buildings as another shot rang out, busting the café sign. In a matter of seconds, the beast was thundering at a breakneck pace across the open ground. Marvin found a gap and fired a few more shots in Claiborne's direction but to no avail. He dropped his head in disgust and looked up the street toward where the bodies laid.

Marshal Claiborne rode for the Barkhouse homestead as if the hounds of Hell were pursuing him. He didn't know if anyone was coming after him, but he aimed to beat them to his destination if they were.

Talmadge was sitting outside with a rifle across his lap when he saw his friend coming in a rush.

"Get ready, boys!" he alarmed his sons, who laid in wait inside the house in case they had unwanted visitors.

As the marshal drew closer, Talmadge saw the grisly sight of blood covering his clothes and panicked. Without knowing exactly had happened, Talmadge assumed he was a dead man riding.

"Aaron, you're shot!" he yelled as the horse skidded to a stop.

Exhausted like his horse, Aaron could only shake his head.

"Not my blood," he managed as his wind returned to him.

"Anybody follow you?"

"Don't believe so."

Talmadge scanned the terrain toward Langston as Aaron regained his breath. Augustus came out and took Aaron's horse away to be cared for. Aaron finally stood up straight and looked to Talmadge.

"It's on now," he informed him. "I killed three of 'em."

Talmadge's eyes bulged in disbelief.

"Do you know who?" he asked.

"Older fella named Cook."

"Gene?"

"Uh huh. Cole's boy too"

"Preston?!"

"Yep."

Talmadge couldn't believe his ears.

"Who else?"

"The sheriff."

Talmadge was beside himself. That Aaron had killed three men single-handedly didn't surprise him. It was the fact that he had managed to kill three who were so close to Murphy. Now Talmadge believed this would escalate faster than he had even imagined.

Word of what happened in town made its way to Murphy shortly after it went down. Marvin sent one of the clerks from his store to inform him while he and Melvin gathered the bodies out of the street.

"You sure it was those three?" he'd asked the boy. "Preston, Gene, and Milo?"

"Yes sir."

"And they're all dead?"

His voice held both knowing and disbelief all at once.

"Yes sir," the clerk replied again.

"Thank you for coming to tell me," Murphy said without a flicker of life. "You run on back to the store now."

Murphy wouldn't have known if the boy was still standing there staring at him or if we was already back in town. His body stood at the front door of his house, but his mind was a million miles away.

For the rest of the evening, Murphy was in a trance-like state. The only coherent demand he had made was that Preston's body be made right and laid out on the bed in his room. Getting his lifeless body up the stairs and into his bedroom was not an easy task, but it was asked of them by their boss and Murphy Cole's men didn't dare let him down.

While all of this was taken care of, Murphy wandered off on foot. He didn't even wear a gun, just left himself at the mercy of whom or what may seek to harm him. His men had begun to worry when dark fell, but not long after, he came walking through the door.

"Is he in his room?" was all he asked when he came in to no one in particular.

Dallas Hildebrand was the closest of Murphy's men to him, so he spoke up.

"Yes sir, just like you asked."

His boss didn't even acknowledge that he'd spoken, just went right up the stairs toward Preston's room.

Murphy stopped as he neared Preston's door. He had to take a moment to gather himself. After blowing out a hard breath, he removed his hat and entered the room with his head down. He shut the door behind him but kept his eyes low, still unable to face his dead son.

Finally, he looked at the body that lay stretched out on the bed, arms crossed on his chest and eyes closed. The sight was almost more than Murphy could bear. Tears welled up in his eyes and a lump formed in his throat.

Deep down, he knew this was his boy. He was sure of it, but he didn't look like Preston.

His teeth and jaw were demolished from the bullet that entered just below his nose. You could see into the hole in his forehead and Murphy didn't dare lift his head off the mattress to see what the back of it looked like.

When he could make his legs work again, Murphy shuffled over to a chair that sat beside Preston's bed. Upon sitting down, he only stared at the floor with his hat in his hands. He just couldn't stand the thought of taking in that sight again.

Murphy's anguish quickly turned to anger as he thought about what had been done to his son, brother, and top hand. And all at the hands of that little runt bastard Claiborne. In one fell swoop he had taken the thing that was most precious to him in the world and two of his closest confidants. All in the name of law and order, hiding behind a marshal's badge.

But it wasn't just Claiborne that did it. Worse, he was just a tool that Talmadge Barkhouse was using to do his dirty work. That gutless coward didn't have the nerve to come at him like a man. He didn't know why the marshal was helping Barkhouse, but he hated them both for it. Why couldn't he just take his medicine and lie down like Giles Kayser? His boy had been killed too, but he knew better than to come after Murphy Cole.

Barkhouse's lawman was making him overly confident. Murphy was seething, his heart pounding and chest heaving as if the objects of his hatred stood before him.

This time wouldn't be like Texas, Murphy had promised himself.

Law might have been able to push him north before, but it wouldn't happen again. He'd built this outfit from the ground up and nobody but nobody was going to take it from him. He aimed to have a stranglehold on the cattle business in these parts no matter who had to die. The only two people he knew for sure would have to meet that fate at this point were Talmadge Barkhouse and U.S. Marshal Aaron Claiborne. He owed that to his boy.

Once he calmed himself down to a simmer, the hurt began to flood back in on Murphy. With his left land, he blindly reached over and grasped the cold hand of his only son.

"They'll pay for this son. I promise you," he said. "They'll pay with their lives."

He dropped his hat and his son's hand and buried his face in his own.

Then Murphy Cole wept. He wept for his boy. He wept for his brother. He wept for one of his best friends. He wept for what he had brought upon them, but he did not weep for what he planned to do to the men who killed them.

When he felt he'd cried all the tears he had in him, Murphy wiped his eyes, picked up his hat, and stood to his feet. Without looking at Preston anymore, he headed for the door.

As he left the room and closed the door behind him, Murphy Cole promised himself he'd shed the last tear he'd ever shed.

# Chapter Nineteen

Just as day broke the following morning, Milo Cole's three deputies headed for the Barkhouse ranch. They hadn't waited around for instructions from Murphy as they were told, but decided they were going to arrest the man who was responsible for their boss' demise.

Almost simultaneously, Warren Clement and Roger Nelson pitched the idea. Both of them were bound and determined, but Jasper Maxwell wasn't sold on their plan.

"Don't you think we owe it to the man?" Warren asked him.

"But Murphy said," he rebutted.

"To hell with Murphy," Roger added. "We don't work for him."

They all knew that this wasn't really true. Though Milo had been their figurative boss, Murphy was in total control of everything the Cole family did. Until now that was.

Talmadge was lying motionless in bed, but was wide awake. The sun was barely filling the sky and everyone else in the house appeared to be asleep. His mind was racing a mile a minute as he tried to figure out what the next move might be. As it turned out, he was not the only one who was awake.

"Talmadge! Talmadge!" he heard from the loft of the barn where Aaron had insisted on sleeping.

Talmadge knew that Aaron wouldn't call him for no reason. He leapt from his bed and threw his pants on over his night clothes, grabbing a rifle as he headed for the door.

"Get up and get right!" he yelled back to the boys.

Aaron was coming up beside Talmadge with his revolver as he emerged from the house.

"Three riders coming," Aaron said, pointing in their direction.

"Any idea who it is?" Talmadge asked as he squinted that way.

Aaron had his telescopic looking glass out trying to get a better look. Right away, he recognized Jasper Maxwell.

"One on the far left is the deputy," he said. "I seen him at the jail when I talked to Cole."

"It's all three deputies," Chauncey remarked, having taken a look for himself with the instrument.

"Could be more men coming. Stay sharp," said Aaron.

The riders never changed their pace as they approached. They just rode up nice and easy within 10 paces or so. Aaron and the Barkhouses half expected them to start shooting without saying a word.

"We're here to arrest Aaron Claiborne," Warren Clement declared.

"On what charges?" Talmadge asked.

"For murdering Gene Cook, and Preston and Milo Cole."

Everyone knew that all this talk was a waste of time. At some point, somebody was going to start shooting.

"You see him do it, Clement?" Talmadge pushed.

"No, but we got witnesses."

"You don't even know what he looks like, do you?" Chauncey chimed in.

Talmadge might have snickered if the moment hadn't been so intense. It was true, Warren didn't know Aaron from Adam, or anybody else for that matter. He'd better hope he knew what he was capable of though.

"I know what he looks like," Jasper Maxwell piped up, pointing at Aaron. "That's him."

Aaron perked up a bit and looked at Jasper, acting as if he'd just recognized him from somewhere.

"Oh, yea. You were at the jail that day I spoke to Murphy Cole," he said.

"That's right."

"Then you remember what I told him, don't you?"

Jasper shuffled uneasily in his saddle as he thought about what Aaron had told Murphy the consequences would be if he didn't take his offer. The proof that he meant business had been displayed right out in the street in Langston. Jasper couldn't make his eyes meet Aaron's, he just answered quietly as he looked straight ahead.

"Uh huh."

"You boys work for Murphy Cole," Aaron said flatly.

Warren Clement was about to speak up, but he didn't have time. Aaron shot him dead right out of his saddle without another word.

He didn't figure they had much to discuss at this point. He'd plainly stated what his intentions were and they'd aligned themselves with the wrong person.

Nobody but Aaron had expected such quick action, not even his cohorts. Jasper had the second quickest reaction to the shooting. Just as soon as Aaron's arm moved in his peripheral vision, he spun his horse around and lit out as fast as he could.

Once he'd gunned down Warren, Aaron turned his gun on Roger Nelson. Roger tried to move, but it was futile. He had two slugs in his chest and was slumping out of his saddle before he could so much as raise the shotgun that had been lying across his lap.

The horses scattered from the shots with nobody to hold them, and the Barkhouses, having regained their senses, fired several rounds in Jasper's direction. They didn't even get close as he'd gotten his horse to top speed in no time and pressed his chest as close to the horse's back as possible to make himself a small, hard-to-hit target.

"That's enough!" Talmadge instructed his boys, knowing they were just wasting bullets.

With the commotion over and two dead deputies lying in front of them, everyone looked to Aaron. He knew they wanted to hear something from him to explain what had just happened, but it was all right there to see.

"It was coming, one way or another," was all he said.

\*\*\*

Jasper Maxwell arrived at Murphy Cole's house at just about the same pace he'd left Talmadge Barkhouse's. He had barely slowed down the whole way and his horse was drawing hard breaths from being pushed so hard.

Toby Wheeler and Harry Bradshaw, two of Murphy's new gun hands, were sitting outside on the porch as he rode up.

"What ails you, boy?" asked Harry, a gruff and well-worn man of about 50.

Jasper hopped down and headed toward them. He was nearly as breathless as his horse.

"Murphy," was all he could manage to say.

Toby and Harry looked at each other, then back at Jasper before Toby got up with a shrug.

"I'll get him."

Toby was probably half Harry's age and clean from head to toe. He was a handsome man, but his soul was as putrid and ugly as it could be. He'd kill anyone or anything if it meant putting a dollar in his pocket. This was just the kind of man Murphy Cole wanted in his employ.

In just a minute, Toby emerged back out onto the porch with his boss in tow. Having a soft spot for animals, Harry had gone to see after the horse Jasper had tried to ride to death.

"Well, what is it boy?" Murphy asked, annoyed.

By now, Jasper had pretty well recovered his breath and could speak plainly.

"That marshal killed Warren and Roger!"

Murphy was stunned. How was this possible? Was he just going house to house killing? Murphy knew he was serious, but this didn't make sense.

"How? When?" he asked Jasper.

"Just now!" Jasper excitedly told him. "I came here fast as I could. Nearly killed my horse."

"Where were you coming from? Warren's place ain't that far from here."

"We weren't at Warren's. We were at the Barkhouse place."

He was about to go on, but Murphy cut him off. This bit of information had not set well with him.

"You were where?"

"At the Barkhouses'."

Murphy's tone appeared to be lost on Jasper, but it was painfully obvious to Toby that he was not pleased.

"What were you doing there?" Murphy continued.

"We went to arrest the marshal."

This sent Murphy over the edge he had been teetering on. He was incensed.

"And who in the hell told you to do that?" he demanded to know.

Now Jasper was well aware of just how angry Murphy was becoming. He began trying to explain himself out of trouble. After all, no one was there to dispute him.

"Well... uh... Warren...uh," he stammered.

"Warren what?" Murphy demanded with a stiff backhand that sent Jasper stumbling back several steps as he tried to maintain his balance.

Jasper wiped the blood from the corner of his mouth and straightened up. Then the truth poured out of him.

"Warren had it in his head we owed it to Milo to get the man that killed him. I told him we was supposed to wait on you, but his mind was made up so we went out there. And that marshal killed both of 'em before they could even get their guns up. Talmadge and his boys were there, but they didn't shoot 'til I was leaving."

This answer told Murphy a lot. First of all, it told him that there had been three men under his command who didn't follow orders and two of them were now dead. Secondly, it told him that this nuisance marshal was proving himself even more to be quite the formidable adversary. And lastly, but perhaps most importantly, it told him that Jasper had somehow escaped a seemingly inescapable situation to bring him this news. Jasper Maxwell was quickly digging himself a deep hole without even realizing he was holding a shovel.

"Did you at least shoot back?" Murphy asked, feigning a calmer demeanor. "Did ya hit anybody?"

It then began to click for Jasper that he was probably in over his head here. He started to think he'd have been better off to just ride clear out of the country instead of coming here. Like his dead boss, he wasn't fit for the position he held. He'd only become a deputy because he was friends with Milo, nothing more. There were no serious issues in and around Langston until Murphy started them. He'd never had to face up to trouble before, and now that he did, he was terrified.

"No, I didn't shoot," he said, barely above a whisper.

"What's that?" asked Murphy mockingly, his hand cupping his ear as if he was trying to hear better.

"I said I didn't shoot. I took off soon as I seen the marshal make his move," Jasper said a little louder.

That was all that Murphy wanted to hear him say.

"So besides not listening to my clear orders, you also ran from trouble?"

"I reckon so."

His voice was once again barely audible.

"What?" Murphy yelled, even startling Toby a bit.

"I reckon so," Jasper repeated.

Murphy was tired. He was tired of his plan not working fast enough and this marshal being a thorn in his side now. His men were dying and it wasn't supposed to be this way. Now this sniveling weasel had pushed him too far. Murphy had had enough. He had to do something this very minute or he felt like he might explode.

"That's it. Kill this piece of shit," he told Toby.

Both Toby and Jasper looked to Murphy as if they were trying to determine if this was a sincere order. When Toby didn't act fast enough for his liking, Murphy glared back at him.

"I said kill him."

The order was sincere alright.

"What? No!" Jasper pleaded.

He tried to pull his pistol, but it was too late. Toby had pulled his own and fired, striking him in the palm he had held up as some sort of ineffectual defense. Toby fired again, hitting him in the upper chest. As Jasper stumbled and fell back off the porch, the other four chambers of Toby's revolver were emptied into his body. His leg kicked weakly a time or two, then he was done.

This was nothing to Toby. He just dumped his empty hulls and reloaded. Harry came running from the stables with his pistol drawn, expecting trouble.

Ed Hughes, Jeremiah Cook, and Dallas Hildebrand had been accompanied by Jose Amaro to check on the herd and were headed back in when they heard the shots. They hurried their pace and rode up shortly after, ready for a fight.

It didn't take long for everyone to realize what all the shots had been about, at least in part. Jasper Maxwell laid dead in the yard in a pool of his own blood while Toby Wheeler stood triumphantly beside his boss with a wad of shell casings littered at his feet. With everyone gathered around and attentive, Murphy took this moment to make a point.

"You see that?" he asked, pointing at Jasper's lifeless body. "He was insubordinate and a coward. You wanna be either of those things and ride with this outfit, you'll get just what he got."

That was just as plain as he could make it. He went back inside as everyone else set about doing what they felt they'd better do, whether it was burying the body, putting up horses, or whatever. At this point, it paid to be busy doing something constructive.

# Chapter Twenty

Montgomery Cole's heart was heavy. He hadn't slept well in months and that insomnia grew worse the longer the ongoing feud between his brother and Talmadge Barkhouse endured. He'd done his best to stay strong and put on a brave face for the people of Langston and his congregation, but chinks were developing in his armor.

He'd lost the majority of his regular church members, not for anything he'd done to run them off, but for fear of being seen as taking sides in the matters between the local ranchers. Talmadge and his family were well-liked by pretty much everyone in and around Langston. Even Murphy Cole may have liked the man if he hadn't been so singularly focused on taking everything he owned away from him.

Even for as much as everyone liked Talmadge Barkhouse though, they feared Murphy Cole even more. When it first got out about what he and his men had done to Asa Barkhouse and Simon Kayser, everyone was shocked. Murphy being less than friendly as he'd always been was no indication of the true evil he was capable of.

Although, if you took a good look at the efforts he'd made to ensure that his brothers held positions of power, his attempt at taking over the cattle trade in the area made a good deal of sense. Still, most people would think an attempted buyout would be the first logical step if this was indeed his plan. Murphy Cole was not like most people though; he preferred to take what he wanted by any means necessary.

Now his brother, the preacher, had to deal with the consequences. All Monty had wanted to do for years was to follow God and make a positive impact on the lives of others. Murphy resented him for this. He hated that his older brother, whom he had looked up to at one time, had chosen the path of the righteous.

Murphy didn't understand how he could possibly want to follow God, much less be a preacher considering the upbringing the Cole boys had. Monty had lived it just like the rest of them had and probably got the worst of it.

Their father had been a preacher, but nothing at all like Monty. Rather than using the position for virtuous reasons, he used it as an excuse to mete out punishment as he saw fit. If he wanted to do something, he could always find a scripture to twist to fit just what he needed. This always included beating his sons mercilessly daily for sometimes nothing more than breathing too loudly. His wife was just as likely to be on the receiving end of one of these beatings as her sons were.

This was one way that Murphy differed greatly from their father. He never laid a hand on Preston as long as he was alive and treated his wife like a queen. The death of her and their second child during childbirth was the final straw for Murphy. At that point he decided there would be no turning to God or anyone else. He was going to make it big and leave an empire to his son.

Just as he was in Langston, Monty was present when Murphy made his first attempt at building his empire through ill-gotten means. Monty had a well-established church in south Texas when Murphy showed up, now a cattleman. Neither of them could quite explain why Murphy decided to follow his brother, but subconsciously he wanted to show his older brother that he could succeed without God.

Murphy had been younger and much more careless then than he was now. He had no real strongholds there and no way of wielding power when he tried to implement some of the same tactics he'd tried on the Barkhouses. When the clues quickly began to point to him, the law was quick to come down hard on him. Feeling the pressure of what his punishment may be, Murphy quickly fled without a single head of cattle and only one member of his outfit, Gene Cook.

After Murphy's fast and hostile exit, pressure began to be put on Monty for his brother's actions. People he had once considered friends now treated him as if he was a leper. They couldn't help but wonder if he had been a part of the bigger picture all along. No one really wanted to believe it, but it did seem plausible. What were the chances that two supposedly estranged brothers would wind up in the same place just before some nefarious activities took place?

Feeling unwanted and mistrusted, Monty took his leave less than a month after his brother. He wandered about for a few years ministering here and there until he found out about the passing of his fellow clergyman in Langston. Upon arriving in Langston and being welcomed with open arms, he felt at peace for the first time in a long time. That peace was shattered when Murphy showed his face in town. He knew that trouble was likely, but the arrival of his other brothers shortly after raised his suspicions even higher. Murphy's installation of their brothers in prominent positions all but confirmed Monty's fears.

Now the chickens had come home to roost. Monty had wanted to warn people about Murphy, but he hoped that his prayers had worked and that he had changed. Instead, he now felt guilt for the turmoil that had befallen his friends. It was all he could do to stand before his diminished congregation on Sundays and preach without feeling like a traitor.

If he thought it would do anything besides make things worse, he'd try to talk to Murphy and convince him to stop what he was doing. The time for that had passed now though. Things that could not be halted were now in

Christopher Reynolds • 188

motion and all he could do was count the bodies. At this point, eulogies had become redundant and funerals were no longer held for fear of attack from the opposite side during a time of weakness.

While his brother was spending much time in prayer and emotional pain, Murphy Cole used his time in a much different way. He was down three more men, one of which was his own doing. Now he couldn't help but believe he'd made a mistake in having Jasper killed. Jasper wasn't a great asset by any means, but he was another body and gun. It was too late for such thoughts though. They still had the numbers advantage and it was time to move on.

On the other side, Aaron Claiborne was eager to strike again. Making fast and harsh moves had served them well so far and the marshal figured that would be their best bet going forward.

The day he'd killed the two deputies, Claiborne and the Barkhouses and Kaysers learned some new information. Tom Walton had taken a risk to ride out and let them know that Cole had hired three gun hands. It wasn't unexpected, but knowing what you're facing up to is always advantageous. According to Tom, the men had been in town and weren't shy about telling people why they were there.

"Good," was Aaron's response.

The others looked at him as if he was insane. How could this possibly be a good thing?

"If they're that cocky, they'll underestimate us."

"I sure hope you're right," Giles told him, still worried.

"I better get out of here," said Tom. "Just thought y'all should know."

Everyone expressed their gratitude and Tom went on his way. Being a business owner in town right out in front of everybody, they realized how much Tom had to lose in this situation. Especially if things went Murphy Cole's way and he found out that Tom had helped them in any way, Tom and his family were in for a rude awakening. Marshal Claiborne had no intentions of letting that happen though.

"In the morning, we're going scouting," he said.

No one knew exactly what he meant, but they knew it was what they'd be doing.

# Chapter Twenty-One

Aaron Claiborne and his scouting party mounted up bright and early to ride out toward the Cole ranch. He needed to get an idea of how to best make an ambush, and to do so needed to lay eyes on it himself.

He decided to take the young men with him and leave the patriarchs behind to watch out for the women and their homesteads. Aaron, Augustus, Chauncey, Luke, and Daniel headed out to hopefully find the answers they needed.

They began by taking a wide berth of the house, opting rather to swing around and try to find the path of least resistance. They'd covered a good amount of ground and were beginning to get into the edge of the herd when Luke spoke up.

"We got people."

Everyone froze and scanned the area. Sure enough, a few hundred yards due east were four men on horseback. Caught in the wide open, Aaron led his men back over a small rise back the way they'd come from. The crew left their horses long enough to see for sure how many and who they were dealing with. Giving his looking glass over to Luke, Aaron was informed that Jeremiah Cook, Ed Hughes, Dallas Hildebrand, and a fourth man he'd never seen were the riders. It looked to be a Mexican.

"Must be one of those gunmen," Gus remarked.

"Gotta be," Luke agreed. "Cole ain't got any Mexicans that work for him."

They studied the four men as they crouched in the tall grass, passing the looking glass around to take a look.

"Should we go after 'em?" Chauncey asked. "We've got the numbers."

Although he wasn't outright proud of his actions, Chauncey had gained a good deal of confidence by how he'd carried himself in the shooting in town. He felt he'd done good and his father told him as much. Aaron was less confident in this crew, but didn't want to be too obvious about it at the risk of hurting morale.

"I don't know," he said. "I'd like to get to their boss first. Cut the head of the snake off and the body can't hurt you."

This made enough sense to them. As a group they decided to circle back to get Talmadge and Giles before riding on Murphy Cole's homestead. With any luck, they hadn't been seen and would have an even bigger advantage while these four were away.

That was not the case though.

Dallas had spotted the five of them as soon as they originally crested the hill they'd done their looking from and warned the others. Carefully, without giving themselves away, they'd kept an eye on them and waited for them to make their move. As soon as they were gone, Jose spoke up.

"We need to go back. With us gone, they'll go back for the boss."

His accent was thick, but his English was impeccable. No one bothered to disagree with him and they rode hard for home.

Amaro had pegged Claiborne's thinking dead on the money. They were both very qualified for the positions they held. It would soon be time to see who was better.

\*\*\*

A short while later, Aaron, the Barkhouse men, and the Kayser men sat on horseback along the edge of a slight plateau that was situated in front of Murphy Cole's home. It was a couple hundred yards to the front fence from where they would soon begin their onslaught.

Even though he wasn't happy to be in an imminent fight, Giles was happy that he had made the decision to stand by his longtime friend. Aaron was happy to be there as well, but he was almost looking forward to the fight. This was the kind of thing he was good at and helping a friend made it all the better. He ran through a few quick instructions before they made their break.

"Stay on your horse until you see me get off mine if you can help it," he instructed. "It'll keep you mobile and give you a little more protection."

Everyone nodded. Talmadge and Giles were battle-proven, but Aaron was much more experienced with a gun. After all, it was his job.

"Outside of that, there ain't much to say," Aaron continued. "It's gonna get loud and ugly quick. People are gonna bleed and die. And not just them."

These words really made the weight of what they were about to do sink in. It was a harsh sentiment, but true as true could be. This was no light matter.

Aaron took a look to either side at his comrades a final time and gave a nod. With that, they took off, approaching the house at a gallop.

With their guns at the ready, the seven of them sailed over the fence and into the yard. Aaron slowed up a bit after doing so and the others followed suit. Something didn't seem exactly right so he wanted to be cautious. They were well within a hundred yards of the house now that they were inside the fence.

The group spread out and eased forward as shots rang out from inside the house. One of the first bullets found it's mark in Talmadge's gut. He leaned on his horse to keep from falling off and cut toward the right of the house.

Another bullet drilled Daniel's horse in the neck, taking it off its feet. Daniel narrowly escaped being crushed under its weight and took cover behind the body of his fallen beast.

As quickly as he could, Aaron took off for the back of the house. As he went, he caught a glimpse of someone in a window and fired, splattering glass shards all over Ed Hughes.

Bullets continued to fly until Cole's men had to reload. Recognizing this lull in the pace, Giles leapt from his horse onto the front porch and made a dash for the front door, only to find it locked. Two quick blasts from his shotgun to the locking mechanism blew it open and granted him entry. Rolling on his right side as he drew his pistol from the same hip, Giles made it inside. The already bloodied Hughes was frantically loading his rifle when Giles spotted him. His first shot missed, but his second caught Ed directly in the throat.

By now, Aaron had gotten in the back door and was working his way to the front. He and Giles both laid eyes on Jose at the same time, filling him full of lead as he slumped against the wall.

Giles got up to his feet and quickly jammed some new cartridges into his pistol. He and Aaron looked around and at each other trying to figure out where their other adversaries were. To their surprise, more shots erupted outside.

Without being detected, Jeremiah Cook and Harry Bradshaw had slipped outside after Aaron came in and were exchanging fire with Augustus and Luke, who were still on their horses. Bullets were whizzing everywhere and not hitting their mark. Gus rode right up on Jeremiah and was prepared to fire when the hulking man snatched him out of his saddle. As he slammed on his back, Gus lost the handle on his gun. Choosing to use his pistol as a club instead of shooting it, the brute laid into Gus. Gus squirmed and fought as hard as he could, but he was physically outmatched. Jeremiah slammed the butt of his pistol into

Gus' head repeatedly until he laid still. All Gus had managed to do was scratch his killer's face.

Seeing his friend being pummeled to death, Luke turned his attention from Harry to Jeremiah. Harry welcomed this though. He was a hired gun, but this was not his preferred form of warfare. With nobody shooting at him, he looked for his horse to get away.

Luke tried to shoot Jeremiah, only to find his cylinder empty. Doing the only thing he could think to do at the moment, he dove off of his horse and onto Jeremiah's broad back. He pounded him in the back of the head, but was quickly flipped onto his own back. Jeremiah struck a couple of blows to Luke's chest before a bullet smacked him in the side of the head and killed him. It was Talmadge, who had gotten around to the back of the house.

Luke was in pain, but relieved as he rolled the limp body off of him. Talmadge's eyes locked onto Gus' mutilated head and tears filled his eyes. He'd lost yet another son. He was soon sobered as a series of shots rang out from upstairs inside. Suddenly, a flash came by the other end of the house headed toward the stables out back. It was Dallas Hildebrand who had decided to go the route of Harry Bradshaw.

Having eased down off of his horse, neither the injured Talmadge nor Luke were in a position to pursue. Dallas was on his way quickly. Chauncey had gotten back in the saddle and gave chase, shooting a few times, but to no avail.

In a few minutes, Aaron and Giles came out of the back door to meet up with the others and see who was left standing.

"Something ain't right," Aaron proclaimed as he emerged from the house. "Murphy ain't here."

When the shooting outside had subsided, Aaron and Giles had decided to search the house to try and find who else might be around. Dallas was the only man they found.

He'd managed to escape by laying down a barrage of fire as they entered the room and slipping out of his window.

Giles was the first one to realize that Talmadge was bleeding.

"Talmadge, you're hit!," he exclaimed.

"Gus is dead," Talmadge said, looking down at his dead son and ignoring his own pain.

Everyone then stopped to take inventory of where everyone else was. Chauncey had come riding back and they were all accounted for except Daniel.

"Where's Daniel?" Giles asked.

Nobody knew, but a quick search answered their question. He was lying by his horse right where he had been for majority of the conflict. He was dead though. At some point before he made his escape, a bullet from Dallas' rifle had exploded Daniel's heart. Giles dropped to his knees and held his son's dead body.

While the others were busy being happy to be alive and mourning the two who had died, Aaron couldn't help but think.

"Didn't that Walton fella say that Cole had hired three gun hands?" he asked.

"Yea," Talmadge answered weakly from the loss of blood.

"Me and Giles killed that Mexican, but that's the only one I seen."

"One took off," Luke offered.

Aaron mulled it over. Something wasn't sitting right with him. These men were waiting for them. Murphy and his brothers not being there didn't seem too odd, but surely he wanted his gunmen here for this. Maybe the other one was tasked with protecting Murphy, but it still didn't feel right.

"Y'all need to check on your women. I got a bad feeling," he said. "Me and Chauncey will take care of things here."

No one else had really thought about it until Aaron said something, but it was now a genuine worry. It appeared that there was no low that Murphy wasn't willing to stoop to. Perhaps this was his latest.

As quickly as they could, Talmadge, Giles, and Luke mounted up to go check on their respective wives who were all at their own homes.

"You gonna be alright?" Giles asked Talmadge, concerned about his friend's gunshot wound.

"I'm fine," he replied as powerfully as he could muster.

With this assurance, the three of them left in a hurry.

***

Earlier, when his men had come back with the news that they were being watched by five men, Murphy Cole made some quick decisions. He told everyone to be ready to shoot from downstairs and up and in any direction because, like Jose had pointed out, they would be coming.

The amount of riders also told Murphy something else; Giles Kayser had decided to come to the aid of his friend. It was just as well because he was going after him when was done with Talmadge Barkhouse anyway. He may as well kill two birds with one stone.

Since most or all of the men would likely be at the skirmish, Murphy decided that the wives would be paid a visit. Toby Wheeler was brought along due to his willingness to do anything for money. After telling Toby how to get to the Kayser place, they split up and Murphy headed for the Barkhouses'.

Belle and Judith, and even Claire were no pushovers. They'd spent enough time in dangerous circumstances in years past with the men in their lives to be prepared to defend themselves.

Giles and Judith had thought it best for their girls to be away from the house just in case of anything hitting close to home due to their youth. Mary and Martha were sent to one of their favorite places to play, a small grove of cottonwood trees with wild growing blackberries scattered intermittently throughout a few hundred yards south of home. As it would happen, Toby's path brought him right by the girls' area of refuge.

Riding along, Toby thought he heard a faint sound from toward the patch of trees. Before he even had to think, his hand was at his hip and instinctively gripping his Remington. He slowed his horse to an easy walk and pointed him toward the cottonwoods. Again Toby heard the noise, but this time he identified it; it was the laughter of a young child.

Silently, he slipped out of his saddle and tied his horse off to a limb. He took slow, easy steps in the direction of the laughter. Within 30 yards of the tree line, he spotted the source of the laughs, Mary Kayser. Sick thoughts in his mind, Toby purposefully stepped on a stick, cracking it and alerting the young girl to his presence.

Mary, the only one of the girls that he could see, whipped her head around quickly at the cracking of the stick. The big, playful smile quickly left her face. Her parents had warned her and her sister of bad men coming to harm them and right away she knew that this was one of those bad men. She let out a scream and turned to run once she could make her legs move, but was quickly met with a bullet in her tiny back. This brutal less-than-human scoundrel had taken the life of a nine year-old girl for no real reason other than he wanted to.

Martha had been hiding as part of the game that she and her sister had been playing, but came out of hiding when it seemed her older sister was taking too long to come find her. Unfortunately, she came out just soon enough to watch the bad man shoot her sister. She let out a small yelp, but it obviously went unheard. Not knowing what to do, the frightened little girl curled up in the fetal position in some undergrowth.

After replacing the spent round in his cylinder, Toby went over and kicked Mary's lifeless body, rolling her over. Her bloodstained dress brought a sadistic smile to his face. This sick individual was doing anything for money, but more than that, he was enjoying it.

He took a quick survey of the area, but seeing or hearing nothing out of the ordinary, headed back to his horse. When his footsteps faded from hearing, Martha ran as fast as her little legs would take her home.

*** 

Arriving at his own home, Talmadge found the front door standing wide open. Right away he knew this was not a good sign at all. Adrenaline pumping, he willed himself down from his horse and stumbled inside.

"Belle! Belle!" he hollered out to no response.

There was definite signs of struggle inside and Belle was nowhere to be found. The dining table and chairs had been knocked around and their dishes were strewn about. After checking the other rooms, he came back and noticed a fresh bullet hole in the wall. Looking down, he noticed the pistol he'd left with Belle lying on the floor. He checked and its cylinder and found a spent cartridge hull. His woman may have been taken, but she had fought back.

Talmadge was suddenly disoriented from the blood loss and bending over to pick up the gun. He shuffled around unsteadily and found himself a seat in one of their chairs. He told himself he'd sit there long enough to regain his bearings, then he'd go look for Belle.

Not sure if he'd maintained consciousness all the while, Talmadge looked up toward the door and found it filled with Murphy Cole's hefty form.

"Looking for somebody?"

Talmadge started for his pistol, but was quickly advised not to.

"Uh uh," said Murphy as he wagged his finger at the injured man.

Seeing that Murphy had his own gun at the ready, Talmadge figured he'd better oblige. At this point he didn't care about dying. The thought of his own death didn't faze him, but he needed to know where his wife was.

"Where is she?" he growled at Murphy.

"She who?" Murphy asked mockingly.

Talmadge was in no mood for these games. He'd been angry for a long time, but he was nearly defeated now.

"I'm tired, Murphy. Now where's my wife?"

Murphy tilted his head and took a good look at Talmadge. It made him almost giddy to see Talmadge in such poor condition.

"Yea, you don't look so good. You need a doc?"

The room was spinning for Talmadge and he was doing everything he could to stay awake and focused.

"It's enough," he muttered. "Where's Belle?

"Oh, Belle," Murphy said as if he just now realized who Talmadge had been referring to. "I've got her tucked away somewhere nice and safe."

Talmadge didn't like the prospect of Belle being anywhere that Murphy had taken her at all.

"Let her go. Please," he said desperately.

Murphy was actually caught off guard by this response. He enjoyed having the power though.

"Please? Why that almost sounds like begging."

"Whatever it takes," Talmadge said weakly. "I'm tired of burying my family."

"Then just die," Murphy said flatly.

Talmadge looked up and directly into Murphy's eyes.

"Okay," was all he said.

Once again, Murphy was taken aback.

"Huh?"

"Kill me," Talmadge said as sternly as he could. "Just let the rest go."

This proposition seemed to interest Murphy.

"How would that work?" he asked.

Talmadge knew he wasn't long for the world and was using whatever bargaining power he thought he might have left.

"I don't know," Talmadge replied. "Find some paper, put it in writing. Bring 'em here and I'll tell 'em. Just let them leave in exchange for my life."

Now Murphy was really intrigued. Talmadge was handing him what he'd wanted all along right there. Talmadge couldn't know his intentions or anything he'd done, so he went along with it.

"That's all you want?" he asked "For them to be able to leave?"

Talmadge nodded.

"Alright, I'll make that deal," Murphy smiled. "I gotta tell you, I never thought..."

Murphy was cut short by the thundering of a Colt revolver. His head snapped back as the bullet entered at base of his skull, killing him instantly. The pistol fell from his hand as he collapsed to his knees and then onto his face in a heap. The life left his eyes as quickly as the bullet left the barrel of the gun.

Talmadge looked past the downed body and saw Aaron standing with his revolver in hand. Unbeknownst to either of the negotiating men, he'd snuck up to the front door of the house and taken careful aim on Murphy.

"No!" Talmadge screamed.

This was by far the loudest he'd been able to speak since he'd been shot. He stood uneasily and stumbled toward Aaron angrily.

"He was gonna let them go!" he continued. "And you killed him!"

"No, he wasn't," Aaron said defiantly.

"Yes, he was," Talmadge countered as he grew closer.

He lost his balance and fell forward, but Aaron caught him. He looked into Aaron's eyes, once again fighting to remain conscious.

"I just found Belle. She's dead, Tal."

Aaron may as well have shot Talmadge as to have told him this news. He'd been the one that had left his wife alone and it had cost her life. A flood of thoughts began to pour through his mind. He'd lost nearly all of his family due to his own stubborn pride. Deep down, he knew that a respectable man could not be expected to roll over and give up what was his, but he was not thinking rationally.

Instead, he could only see the images of his dead sons in his mind's eye. He couldn't help but wonder what kind of shape his poor wife's body had been left in by Murphy Cole. His own wound was beginning to come into focus more now. He was hurting so bad he couldn't ignore it and eventually lost the battle with unconsciousness.

\*\*\*

Talmadge was out of it for most of the evening and into the night without so much as a flinch. Aaron and Chauncey would have thought him dead if not for the occasional shallow breaths he took in. Aaron had taken a look at the wound and cleaned and dressed it, but that was the extent of his doctoring ability. Both he and Talmadge's only remaining son knew that this was not a promising situation.

They later learned from Giles that Belle wasn't the only female killed that day. For one reason or another, Toby Wheeler had never showed up at the Kayser home. Martha, though, had come running home telling them of some bad man that had killed Mary in their special playing place. They thought that surely she was making this story up since she and her sister had been warned so fervently about the bad men who might come.

A quick trip to the cottonwood grove proved otherwise though. There they found their little girl dead of a gunshot wound. It was then the Kaysers' turn to question their every decision. At the time, keeping the girls away from the house had seemed wise, and in all actuality, it should have been. Toby was on his way to their house when pure, dumb, bad luck led him astray. They had no way of knowing this though. They also couldn't help but question getting involved in the first place. The time for those thoughts was unfortunately gone, though.

"It had to be that other gun hand that wasn't at Cole's place," Giles told Aaron. "This was just cruel."

It was all that Giles could do to hold himself together and Aaron could tell.

"Don't you worry," he assured Giles. "I'm gonna find him and take care of it."

"You find him, but I'll handle it myself."

Aaron nodded. Such an ugly thing done to a precious little girl needed to be avenged by her father. He'd do everything in his power to make sure Giles got that opportunity. For now their conversation turned to other matters.

"I don't think he'll live long," Aaron said in reference to Talmadge.

"Don't look good," Giles agreed. "What do we do next?"

"I don't know just yet. It ain't over though."

"You're damn right it ain't over," Giles said with an uncharacteristic menace. "Some of them are still breathing."

Even under such extenuating circumstances, it was surprising to hear Giles speak in such a manner.

"And I just killed their boss so it ain't over for them either," Aaron added.

"Maybe they'll be ready to end it soon then."

"Maybe so."

# Chapter Twenty-Two

Aaron stuck around long enough the next morning to see that Talmadge was alive and Chauncey was awake before he headed out to take care of the business he had for the day. He'd decided to take the calculated risk of riding into Langston to deliver the corpse of Murphy Cole to his brother Montgomery.

He knew that Marvin and Melvin Cole, as well as whoever may be left of Murphy's crew may be there, but he wanted to bring Murphy's body to Montgomery personally. There was also other business he planned to attend to while he was there.

Aaron pulled the wagon up to the back of the church and went in to get Monty.

"You know what that is?" he asked the preacher as they walked around back and he pointed at the wagon's covered load.

Monty looked from Aaron, to the wagon, and back to Aaron. A pained look covered his face.

"I've got an idea," he said.

He'd heard there'd been a wild shootout at his brother's house and Aaron's presence here told him all he needed to know.

"You wanna look?" Aaron asked.

"Reckon I better."

Monty stepped forward and hesitantly peeled back the covering, revealing Murphy's body. He only looked briefly. It was all he needed and all he could bear.

"So what now?" he asked Aaron, dejected.

"Well I figure your brothers and whatever's left of Murphy's outfit won't be too happy about this."

Monty barely acknowledged Aaron's answer as he just stared at the back of the wagon where his dead brother lay.

"You alright?" Aaron asked.

As soon as he asked, the marshal felt like a fool for having done so. Despite the man Murphy Cole might have been, he was still Monty's brother.

"I'm not surprised it came to this," Monty said. "But it's strange seeing him like this. Almost like I thought he'd never die."

Monty had been through the loss of his brother Milo at the hands of this same man, but this was different. It wasn't that he'd delivered Murphy's body to him, but rather how he'd felt tied to him for so long. Now that those ties had been severed, he somehow felt more bound than ever. It wasn't grief that had stricken him, but some other strange, unfamiliar feeling.

Aaron, realizing that he had a lot on his mind, gave the preacher a few more quiet moments of reflection. He was putting himself in danger by being there in town though, so he couldn't wait around too long.

"Anyways," he started. "I just thought you ought to have his body."

Despite the hostility between the parties, this respect shown for Murphy's body was not unusual for Aaron. He and Chauncey had left the bodies of the deceased at Cole's place inside the house so that they wouldn't be bothered by any animals or weather.

Monty finally turned to face Aaron.

"Thank you for that," he said.

Aaron nodded politely, but Monty could tell there was something else on his mind.

"Is there anything else?" he asked.

"Well..." Aaron trailed off.

"Yes?"

"I was wondering if there was any difference in our standing now."

Monty had to think on this for a moment before his mind went back to their conversation in the church a while back and he understood.

"Far as I can tell, we're right where we've always been," he said as he extended his hand.

Aaron nodded and shook the preacher's hand. He helped Monty unload the body and bring it in to the church before quickly leaving to handle the other matter he had left to take care of.

***

"You ready?" Aaron asked Giles as soon as he stepped out of his house to see what brought the marshal there.

Giles seemed perplexed at this question for a moment, but quickly caught its meaning.

"Yea!" he said excitedly. "Let me grab my things."

In just a matter of minutes, Giles was back out, on his horse, and ready to ride.

***

Langston's hotel, now owned and operated by a man by the name of Charles Potts, was a nice enough establishment with neatly decorated rooms and friendly service.

In one of these rooms, Aaron Claiborne sat silently in a chair in a corner waiting for someone. He hadn't been there a terribly long time when just the man he was looking for unlocked the door and stepped inside.

Toby Wheeler was surprised to see the stranger in the corner with a pistol trained on him as he entered his previously locked room. He considered making a break for it, but something, perhaps his cockiness, kept him from fleeing. He hadn't seen Aaron up close to know who he was, but he was beginning to get an idea.

"You Toby Wheeler?" Aaron asked.

"Who the hell are you?" he snapped back.

"I asked you first," said Aaron with a sly grin.

Toby was annoyed at the whole situation and trying to figure his way out of it. Running was still an option. He hadn't closed the door behind him. Maybe he could draw and catch the marshal off guard, but that didn't seem likely so he decided to talk while he figured it out.

"Yea, I'm Toby Wheeler," he said. "Now who are you?"

"It's not me you should be worried about," Aaron responded.

"Huh?"

In a flash, the door behind Toby slammed shut. He heard and saw it happen, but couldn't move fast enough. Giles already had a hold of him and his blade was at his throat.

"You like killing little girls?" Giles asked him harshly.

Aaron winced a little as Giles cut Toby to the bone, slitting his throat and dropping him in a heap on the floor. Mary's killer didn't last long. Giles and Aaron looked down at their handiwork for a moment, but were quickly gone.

Aaron had told Giles that he would deliver Toby to him to kill personally and he did just that. After leaving Montgomery earlier, Aaron set about finding out where Toby might be. After a couple fruitless stops and figuring his target for the type to partake in such activities, Aaron paid a visit to the town brothel. As it turned out, one of the whores had been with Toby a couple of times since he'd been in town and knew what room he was staying in part-time at the hotel. One payment later, Aaron had the information he needed.

As it turned out, it was money well spent.

# Chapter Twenty-Three

The next day found Talmadge a good deal better than he had been the day before, but still not well. Aaron and Chauncey were almost surprised that he had made it this long, but delighted that he had. Still, the prognosis didn't lend itself to a long life post-recovery. In fact, Aaron was pretty sure there wouldn't be a recovery.

For as weak and sick as he was, Talmadge was concerned only for the well-being of the rest of the remaining members of his family. At this point, that didn't just include Chauncey and Claire, but every surviving Kayser and Aaron as well. They'd all been close for years, but this was a deeper connection they had now and he couldn't help but feel responsible for every death that had befallen them. He was now sorry that he just didn't give up and give Murphy Cole what he wanted. He had no idea how they would have made it if he had, but at least they would have been alive.

This was the reason that his every waking moment that he could think straight, he was attempting to devise a plan to save everyone else. He would go along as long as he could be helpful, but he feared that would not be long. When he thought he had a plan that may work, he asked Aaron to gather everyone to hear him out. So that evening, when he felt strong enough to address them, they all came.

He was tearful as he tried to put into words the regret that he felt that it had come down to this.

"I'm just sorry. I really am," was all that he could say that could be understood.

No one in attendance was able to hold back there emotions, even young Martha. They were all grief-stricken, and looking at the shape Talmadge was in, preparing for yet another death. Nonetheless, everyone assured him that this was not his fault and that they supported him. As they'd already reasoned, Murphy had had his eyes on both of their ranches eventually anyway. At least this way they had the opportunity to fight together.

Once they'd composed themselves, Talmadge continued on with his idea.

"The train'll be here Tuesday morning, always is," he said just above a whisper. "I want y'all to be on it when it leaves here."

"What about you, Pa?" Chauncey interjected.

"I doubt I make it that long, son," Talmadge answered him solemnly. "But if I do, I'll be there with you."

Tears flooded Chauncey's eyes at his father's recognition of his own mortality. It was much easier to ignore such a thing when the one whose life was at risk was ignoring it. Talmadge had no time left for false hope. All he could do now was try to save everyone else.

"What about Murphy's brothers? And his men?" asked Giles.

"Chances are they'll have to be fought off. They ain't gonna take this lying down."

"And money?"

"It won't be easy," Talmadge admitted. "We had a little put back you can take. Y'all are gonna have to stick together tight. I need you to help Chauncey."

By now, Talmadge was in tears again, along with Chauncey and Giles.

"Don't you worry about that," Judith assured him.

Chauncey was pretty well grown, and tough, but he had never been on his own, and this was not an ideal time to do so for the first time.

"I can't promise it'll be any easier anywhere else," Talmadge started again. "But a new start has got to be better than this. Maybe y'all can come back after a while, but it'll be hard to be around here regardless of what happens when you leave."

Giles knew he was right. It didn't matter whether they made a clean break, killed the rest of those loyal to Murphy, or whatever else, a town like Langston, despite it's rough patches in the past, was not used to the type of killing that had occurred there lately. They couldn't simply turn their heads from all the blood that had been spilled. That kind of violence weighed heavy on people and that had to be understood.

"I feel like you've felt though, Tal," Giles said. "I hate to leave everything we've worked for, especially after all this."

"Look at me, Giles," Talmadge said as strongly as he'd been able to speak the whole time. "It ain't worth it. Get out with your lives."

He didn't want to hear his best friend speak this way, but Giles understood the reasoning behind it. If anybody had a grasp on when loss outweighed the need to be stubborn, it was Talmadge. He was as strong-willed as anybody Giles had ever known so his giving in held a great deal of sway in Giles' mind.

"I can't think of nothing better," he finally said.

"Good," Talmadge said, genuinely happy that his advice had been heeded. "Unless you think of something better or they bring the fight to us first, that's the plan."

No one was exactly thrilled about this plan, but they didn't have any viable alternatives either. They had from Friday to Tuesday to come up with something else or they'd tentatively be leaving on the weekly train.

Before long, everyone headed home as it was getting late and Talmadge was growing weaker by the minute.

With everyone else gone, Talmadge turned to Aaron, who hadn't said a word the whole time.

"What do you think?" he asked.

"It might work, might not," Aaron replied. "It's better than not having a plan at all."

"You don't sound so sure about it."

"I don't know, Tal," he shrugged.

Aaron couldn't think of any better options at the time, but he was more worried about his friend's health. Death was a normal aspect of his life, but losing a friend like this was a different story. It was at this very moment that he knew that Talmadge would never leave Langston on that train.

*** 

The Barkhouse home was not the only venue that hosted a meeting during those days in the aftermath of the latest shootout.

Melvin, being the oldest of the remaining Cole brothers other than Montgomery took over as a de facto leader. His first act after the burial of their fallen was to call a meeting to regroup, even inviting his older brother. Monty turned down the offer, choosing to continue his vow to not be involved in any violence. After all, that's exactly why Melvin, Marvin, Dallas, and Harry were there.

"I think you all know why we're here," Melvin told them.

Everyone nodded solemnly. Their losses were beginning to get the best of the group and hang heavy on their ever-sinking morale.

"We've got to figure out how to end these damn people," he continued. "They've got more than their fair share of our blood."

Dallas was fired up and tired of being outmatched. It was his opinion that they should have been able to dispense of those simple ranchers long ago. Sure that marshal was more than capable with a gun, but he was still only one man.

"I say we go kill the lot of them right now! They won't know we're coming like we did when they came for us," he offered voraciously. "They're probably all huddled together at the Barkhouses'."

"And if they're not?" Melvin countered. "Who's to say one of them won't slip out and tell the others? Then we'll be caught in an ambush."

Dallas was adamant that his plan would work. He'd had enough of Cole orders not working.

"We'll make sure they don't," he snapped back. "And if they do, we'll be ready for them."

"Being ready didn't do you much good last time," Melvin returned condescendingly.

At this insult, Dallas sprang to his feet in anger.

"What would you know of it anyway?" he asked in reference to Marvin and Melvin not being present for any of the gun fighting.

Harry was in agreement with this, rising to his feet as well.

"Yea!" he added enthusiastically. "Where were you when we were trying to keep from getting our damn heads blown off?"

Now Melvin jumped up from his seat and pointed his finger right in Dallas' face.

"We were doing what Murphy told us to do, same as you!"

Dallas brushed his hand aside and the two came nose to nose, both snarling and red-faced like two rams about to butt heads.

"Well your brother's dead now," Dallas barked at Melvin. "So he can't protect you no more."

The tension in the room was palpable. Something was about to give and everyone could feel it coming. Melvin was ready to explode and make a move after this latest comment. Dallas was just waiting for the slightest inkling that it was about to happen. Sensing this, Harry began to ease around the table, preparing to second Dallas. When it felt as if the bubble were just about to burst, Marvin finally stood and spoke for the first time in the meeting.

"Hold on! Wait a minute!" he proclaimed.

He lightly nudged Harry back with his shoulder and wedged himself between Melvin and Dallas.

"What are we doing here?" he asked. "This ain't the way! It won't accomplish a thing in the world."

All three of the other men loosened up a bit and listened to see where he was going with this.

"If we're gonna go at each other like a bunch of animals, we might as well do them a favor and pull our guns and blow each other to bits right here."

His words were hard, but true. They knew that their infighting was doing nothing but damage. Emotions were high though.

"Now," Marvin went on. "We're all here because of Murphy, for one reason or another. Be it blood, loyalty, or money, that's why we're here. So let's cool off tonight and talk about this in the morning."

All four men took glances around at one another, wanting peace, but not sure if the others felt the same. Marvin had one more thing to say.

"We can do that or we can end this all right here. That's your choices."

He said it with such conviction that no one questioned it. Instead, they all left the room separately without a word, eyeing each other suspiciously the whole way. There was no way to ensure that this unit wouldn't implode, but Marvin had held it together for at least one more night.

# Chapter Twenty-Four

Monday afternoon was the end of the line for Talmadge. His breathing had been labored all through the previous night and that morning to the point that they thought he was gone a few times already.

Upon coming back in from shoring up a few things a little after 1 P.M., Aaron found Chauncey and Claire sitting quietly by their father's bed. Chauncey turned and gave him a telling look.

"He's cold."

Aaron nodded his head and went back outside. The usually stoic marshal had to choke back tears as he left the room. He knew that he had just lost one of the finest friends a man could have. He was truly heartbroken.

When the Kaysers were made aware of Talmadge's passing, they all came together for a quick, quiet funeral, fitting of the man. Talmadge was laid to rest beside the love of his and faithful companion, Belle.

After the service, they all knew that they needed to follow on with his plan. It was the best option they had and Talmadge had done his best to guide them so far. In the morning, they would make their break from Langston.

***

Tuesday morning found the remaining members of the Kayser-Barkhouse clan, as well as U.S. Marshal Aaron Claiborne waiting at the train station for the 9:30 A.M. train. Luke, as he usually did, kept watch over the ladies inside while Aaron, Chauncey, and Giles spread out outside to watch for potential trouble.

Despite their early arrival and careful approach, their presence in town was nothing if not conspicuous. It didn't take long for people around town to notice them and start spreading the news. Dallas Hildebrand was having breakfast in the cafe when he overheard two men discussing the goings-on down at the depot. Obviously, his interest was immediately piqued.

"What's that you say?" he asked the man who seemed to have most of the information.

"The Kaysers and that Barkhouse boy are...," he started, trailing off as he realized who he was talking to.

He knew just as well as everyone else around that Dallas had worked for the late Murphy Cole. This information could be damning for Cole's enemies. Dallas just stared at the man as if instructing him to continue on with his story. Catching his drift, the man continued nervously.

"They're do... down at the train station," he stammered. "Said they were gonna leave on the 9:30."

"You sure about that?" Dallas asked.

"That's what everybody's saying," he replied with a hint of fear.

"Thank you sir."

Dallas quickly left his meal and headed out to round up the others. This was their opportunity and he knew it. Whether these people were leaving or not, this issue had gone past letting them leave without a fight. Soon, Murphy Cole's men would be forcing the issue and seeking retribution for the death of their commander.

Meanwhile, Aaron was taking an annoyed watch by the depot. He didn't like waiting when he knew that fighting was imminent. He was a patient man otherwise, but not being in control of when guaranteed conflict would commence was not his strong suit. If he had it his way, he'd take to fight to them, but there was no way of knowing how and where to find them all.

Marvin was already at his store and easy to find for Dallas.

"They're at the depot, planning on leaving on a train this morning," he said as soon as he walked through the doors.

"Who?" a bewildered Marvin asked.

"You know who."

"Oh."

"Exactly. Have your guns ready and waiting when I get back. I'm going to get Melvin and Harry."

As soon as the words had left his mouth, Dallas headed for the Cole ranch to do what he'd said he was going to do.

At the depot, Chauncey was just as anxious about waiting as Aaron was. He eased toward the marshal and made a little conversation.

"I don't like all this waiting," he remarked.

"Me either," Aaron agreed. "I reckon it's our only choice though."

Soon, Giles joined in as well.

"You think they're gonna come?" he asked as he came up alongside them.

"Oh they'll come," Aaron assured him. "I guarantee they know we're here by now."

"Is it bad that I'm ready for them to get here?"

"If it is, we're both wrong," Aaron told Giles.

The train was making its way into the station as they spoke, screeching to a halt. There wouldn't be many, if any passengers getting off here, but there would be some freight to be unloaded. And at 9:30, they hoped to be leaving on it. As the train made its arrival in Langston, so did Melvin and Harry.

Along with Dallas, they'd come to Marvin's store, armed and ready to do battle.

"How we gonna work this?" Harry asked.

Murphy had hired him and his loyalty now fell with Melvin and Murphy since they had control of the money and he was promised an increase in pay for staying on to finish the job even though Murphy was dead.

"I say we go right at 'em, but spread out," Melvin started. "What do y'all think?"

He was no commander in battle. He'd never been in many tight spots, and definitely not one as severe as this. The same could be said for his brother. They would have to rely heavily on the experience advantage that Dallas and Harry had over them.

"It ought to work I reckon," said Dallas. "Me and Harry will go up either side of the street and y'all go around behind the buildings down either side. Maybe we'll get 'em in a crossfire."

"Everybody alright with that?" Melvin asked.

They all nodded in agreement and prepared to head out. As they did, Melvin grabbed an extra shotgun.

"You taking two shotguns?" Marvin asked him.

"I'm gonna stop by the church," he replied. "Monty ought to part of this too. Murphy was just as much his brother as he was mine or yours. Not to mention Milo."

Marvin didn't say much, but he knew that the chances of his brother joining them were slim to none, even if he was threatened. Say what you want about the man, but he was devout.

Finally, they set out, with each man carrying at least two guns. Marvin and Harry crossed the street to the north side with Marvin cutting through an alley and around the backside of the buildings. Dallas started up the near sidewalk and Melvin took his route toward the back of the church.

Without them noticing, Tom Walton had come from his shop and was making his way determinedly toward the train station with a rifle in his hands. Aaron spotted him and pointed him out to Giles.

"You know that fella with the rifle?"

He felt sure that this approaching man had something to do with their situation, but he didn't know how.

"That's Tom Walton," Giles told him. "He's a friend."

"I reckon you need to go see what he's doing."

Giles nodded and went to meet him on the sidewalk.

"Morning, Tom. Where you headed with that rifle?"

"I come looking for you, Giles. They're coming to kill y'all. They're down at Marvin's store getting ready."

"Well I appreciate the information," Giles told him with a friendly slap on the shoulder.

Tom gave him a strange look.

"What is it, Tom?"

"I'm staying here to help you," he replied.

Giles was surprised by this answer.

"I can't let you do that."

"Don't reckon you got a choice."

As much as Giles appreciated Tom's friendship and offer, he had to figure out a way to make him understand why he couldn't accept it. Just him coming to warn them could be taken badly by some people in town. If things didn't go their way there, he knew that the Coles could be back in power, and possibly be seen sympathetically for avenging their brothers' murders. It all depended on how you looked at things and was much too complicated to be explained quickly when your life was on the line.

"Look here, Tom," said Giles. "When that train leaves here, I'm gonna either be on it or dead, but you'll be here. If this thing goes bad, you still need to be able to make a living here. Maybe one day when things have cooled off, we'll make it back. Regardless, you've got to take care of your family and I've got to take care of mine. Now I appreciate your offer, but I gotta turn you down."

Tom looked dejected. He wanted to help, but what Giles said made a lot of sense. Not knowing what else to do, he reached for Giles' hand and they shook.

"I wish you the best of luck."

"You're a good man, Tom."

A short time later, Montgomery Cole heard a slamming noise coming from the back of the church and went to investigate. What he found was his brother Melvin standing in the doorway with a shotgun in either hand.

"What are you doing?" Monty asked incredulously, taking notice of the damaged door where Melvin had pried it open.

"You're coming with me, now!" Melvin barked.

"I hardly think so," was the response he got.

Melvin pushed his way inside and forced Monty backwards.

"I'm sure you know they're here, don't you?"

"Who?" Monty asked blankly.

Someone had come by and alerted him to the presence of Giles and the others. Expecting gunfire at any time, he'd spent the time since he'd found out in prayer. At this point all he could do was hope and pray for a miracle. His brother barging in and demanding that he come with him while heavily armed was not something he'd expected.

"You know who I'm talking about. Now, here," Melvin snapped as he shoved one of the shotguns into his arms.

Monty wouldn't take the gun and backed away from his brother while shaking his head vehemently.

"I'm not getting involved," Monty declared. "I've stayed out of this all along and I intend to be that way until it's over."

Melvin began closing the distance on his brother again, forcing him backward into the sanctuary.

"Maybe that's part of the problem!" he screamed at Monty. "Maybe if you'd been more involved instead of trying to protect your friends, our brothers wouldn't be dead."

"That's hardly fair," Monty retorted. "Murphy went after them!"

Melvin was having none of this slandering of his deceased brother. He shoved Monty hard with one shoulder and handed him a shotgun again.

"Now you take that!" he ordered.

Feeling as if he had no choice, Monty reluctantly took the shotgun. He didn't move a step though, only stared back at his brother.

By the train, Aaron was trying to keep an eye on both sides of the tracks in case of an attack either way. He stepped back across and looked toward town. His eyes immediately locked on Harry Bradshaw as he eased toward him down the sidewalk to his right. Aaron didn't recognize him as he hadn't seen him face-to-face, but he knew right away that this man meant him harm.

Aaron immediately took a few steps toward him and Harry paused momentarily. This told the marshal all he needed to know. Once again, he walked straight at Harry. Harry had all that he could stand and went for the pistol on his right hip. He had to make the move, but he just wasn't fast enough. He got off one shot, but it went wild as two slugs from Aaron's gun ripped his chest apart. Harry's body hit the ground with a thud and he was done.

Melvin and Monty were still inside the church when the shooting commenced.

"Go!" Melvin demanded as he shoved his brother out onto the front porch.

As they came outside, Aaron looked their way briefly, but turned to look for someone closer as that shot would likely be a waste.

Giles laid eyes on the brothers, but hesitated at the sight of the preacher being there with a shotgun. He knew this didn't seem right and that Monty looked uncomfortable. This created a window of opportunity for Melvin, who pushed his brother aside and leveled his shotgun at Giles. Giles dove to his right as the load of buckshot seared the air where he'd been standing. Melvin fired again, but Giles avoided being hit once more.

"Chauncey!" Aaron yelled as he came back toward the depot.

"Yea?!"

"You and Luke get everybody on the train!"

Chauncey ran to the building to do as he was instructed. Luckily, by now, the train was ready to be boarded. People were running all about trying to avoid being hit as an innocent bystander.

Tucked between two rail cars, Giles could no longer see Melvin. Dallas came into his line of sight though and he stepped out, firing twice as he did. One bullet seemed to have struck Dallas in the leg, but he immediately turned his attention to the man who shot him. With a pistol in each hand, he let out a flurry of wildly inaccurate shots. Giles slid toward the train and fired back. These two shots dealt the death blow to Dallas.

Having both reloaded, Aaron and Giles both went quickly back to the depot.

"I don't know where the brothers are!" Aaron informed him.

"Me either!"

Chauncey and Luke were leading the ladies out of the building and toward the train when a shot rang out to their right. It was Melvin.

"Go back!" Giles screamed, gesturing his family back inside.

Aaron and Giles turned toward Melvin and traded fire with him. Bullets slammed all around the three men until eventually, one lucky shot struck Melvin in the forehead and killed him instantly.

"Y'all need to go," Aaron urged Giles.

Giles waved Luke and Chauncey forward and they came on out. Knowing that they had another Cole to deal with, they made sure to move along quickly. All the ladies had gotten inside, followed by Luke. As Chauncey stepped up, he was met by a bullet ripping quickly through his lower right side.

Luke stepped forward and looked over Chauncey, spotting Marvin with his rifle aimed toward them. In a flash, Luke shouldered the rifle he'd brought along and shot Marvin, who fell to the ground. Everyone seemed shocked that Luke had taken him out. Not that he was ever doubted, but his job had usually been to protect his expectant wife, and often, the other ladies.

Aaron ran over and checked to make sure that Marvin was dead. One bullet from Aaron's pistol later and he was.

Giles was checking Chauncey over as Aaron came back over.

"It's through and through," Giles told Chauncey, Luke, and Aaron.

"Good," said Aaron. "I'm sure they'll have something to patch him up on board. Ask around."

Luke led Chauncey onto the train as Giles stood by Aaron. They both turned their attention to the train's portly conductor who was approaching with an exasperated look on his chubby face.

"What's the meaning of all this?!" he asked, flailing his arms.

Aaron stepped toward him and revealed the badge hidden on his chest by his duster. The conductor's eyes grew exponentially at the sight of the U.S. Marshal's badge.

"It means you've got an injured man on board and I know you've got the supplies to patch him up," Aaron replied. "And it also means if anything happens to any of the folks I just put on this train, I'll be holding you personally responsible. You best believe I'll be checking up on them too. Now get this train out of here!"

"Yes sir," was all he could say as he went back to the head of the train as quickly as he could.

Giles couldn't help but smile as he looked at Aaron. Aaron laughed just a little as he met Giles' look. Their interaction quickly turned much more somber though.

"I can't thank you enough for what you've done," said Giles. "I can never repay you."

"You don't owe me a thing, my friend," Aaron replied.

That was all he had to say. They shook hands firmly and Giles went on in to be with the rest of his family.

Aaron stepped back and looked on as the train prepared to leave. He also took this time to reload his Colt. He didn't plan to use it anytime soon, but that was no reason to leave it anything less than fully loaded.

He hadn't been completely successful in his endeavor of assisting his friends, but the marshal felt that he'd done the best he could. At least he'd been able to get his daughter and grandchild away safely, and with a little luck, the Barkhouse name would live on in Chauncey.

The train's horn bellowed as it let out a cloud of steam and lurched forward. Aaron watched as it left, then saw something on the other side of the tracks that he hadn't expected once it had cleared.

Staring at him from the town side of the tracks with a shotgun in his hands was Reverend Montgomery Cole. Aaron had seen him come out of the church with his brother earlier, but hadn't thought anything of it. So far, he'd been as good as his word and stayed out of the bloodshed, but perhaps the loss of all of his brothers had changed his mind. All Aaron knew for sure was that they both held guns in their hands and this stare was uncomfortable.

For several long moments Monty held Aaron's gaze. Finally, though, he grabbed the barrels of the shotgun with his right hand as he let go with his left and laid it on the ground beside him. This gave Aaron a sense of relief. He hadn't expected to have to exchange fire with the preacher, but he really couldn't be sure. Now he could breathe easy and decided to holster his own gun. It had been used entirely too much during Aaron's time here, but the job was done. He looked once again to the preacher, then turned to go retrieve his horse. The calm and patient beast was waiting for him right where he'd left him, tied up at the back of the train station. The marshal mounted up and left for somewhere he only knew.

Monty watched him as he left briefly, then turned his attention to the four bodies that were strewn about, two of them being his brothers. It was hard to believe that they were all dead now, but he wasn't totally surprised that Murphy's actions had led to harm coming to their brothers. He'd always felt that Murphy's greed and mercilessness was a great burden on their family and he'd been proven right.

People were beginning to spill back out into the street and he was the center of their attention as he took inventory of the carnage and the town that had endured it. It suddenly dawned on him that things were as they hadn't been here in a long, long time. There were no Barkhouses, no Kaysers, and he was the only Cole present. Perhaps they could recover from such violence as they had in the past with him as their moral compass.

Maybe Langston still had a chance. Maybe Montgomery Cole did too.

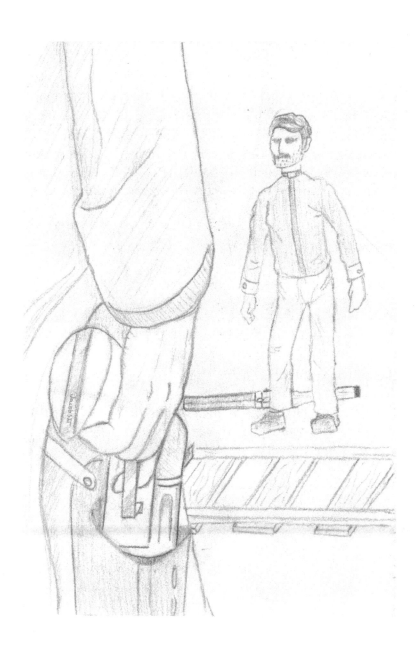

# About Christopher Reynolds

Christopher Reynolds has called rural North Carolina home since his birth in 1993. He graduated in 2016 with a Bachelor degree in Business Management from the University of North Carolina at Pembroke. A lifelong fan of western films and literature, Reynolds cites Louis L'Amour as his favorite author. *Blood on the Range* is his debut novel.

**Social Media**

Facebook:
www.facebook.com/ChristopherReynoldsAuthor

Twitter: www.twitter.com/clreynolds93

**Acknowledgements**

Special thanks to Jacob Sexton for the interior art. To see more of his original art, visit www.instagram.com/jacobsxt.

Made in the USA
Columbia, SC
12 April 2020

91777911R00124